THROAT BABY

By: Author Barbie Amor
Formally known as Barbie Scott

CHAPTER ONE

BAMBI

"Sexy lil' bitch, sexy lil' ho
I love the way you walk, love the way you talk
Let a young nigga come play in your throat
Deep stroke your throat 'til I make you choke
Throat babies, I'm tryna give 'em to you
Throat babies, I'm tryna bust all on you..."

When I fell down into the splits from the top of the pole, the men in the crowd went crazy. It was like a money shower from all the bills that flew through the air. I knew I had racked up at least ten grand or more, and I wasn't done. I lay back on the stage and began to wind my body slowly. I slid my hand into my magic sack while the patrons didn't pay attention, and the moment their eyes landed on my ten-inch dildo, they already knew what it meant. They began cheering me on as I started sucking the tip of it. I seductively teased it and brought up as much spit as I could. The room went silent as if I had them under a hypno. The song changed to Adina Howard's "T-shirt &

Panties," and the lights above changed to red, which meant this was my cue. I went down on the makeshift dick with my mouth until it disappeared down my throat. I had it so far down, I was able to close my mouth with it inside. The lights came on, and the room erupted. So much money was thrown at me it slapped me in the face. I pulled the dildo from my mouth, and they went crazy again. I watched the men with so much confidence because I had done it yet again.

That there, ladies and gents, was how I got the moniker, *Throat Baby*, and no matter how many times I did it, I sent the crowd into a frenzy.

***

"Ms. Davenport, can you explain the difference between Prokaryotic and Eukaryotic? Ms. Davenport!"

"Huhhh—Ohh, my bad, Mr. Fox." I wiped the drool from my mouth and replied to his question. "Prokaryotes are organisms that consist of a single prokaryotic cell. Eukaryotic cells are found in plants, animals, fungi, and protists."

"Thank you." Mr. Fox nodded his head, prolly feeling dumb as hell.

I knew he was only picking on me because I spent most of my days sleeping in his class. It was stupid if you asked me because no matter how much I slept, I was on my shit. I passed every class with flying colors, and I could do this shit with my eyes closed. Literally.

When the bell rang, everyone lifted from their seats to head out. Before I could fly my ass out the door, Mr. Fox called out to me.

"Ms. Davenport, I need you to stay after class."

The few people who were still in the room looked at me. The shit would have been embarrassing had I gave a fuck about what people thought. Therefore, I slid my books into my bag and stepped down to Mr. Fox's desk. He took a seat behind his desk and waited for the last student to leave.

"Why you always picking on me?" I asked him, slightly unbothered. I knew exactly why—I just wanted to hear him say it.

"You know why, Ms. Davenport." He watched me to get my reaction.

I smirked and walked closer to his desk. Damn right, I knew exactly why. I dropped my book bag and kneeled down in front of him. I began to seductively remove his leather belt, then unzipped his pants. He slid his body down in his chair to prepare himself for what he considered a magic trick. I stared into his eyes, and he matched my energy with hunger. I grabbed his dick and began jacking it slowly. When I had him to his hardest extent, I covered it with my mouth and moved both hands behind my back.

"Shiiiit." He grabbed the arms of his seat to keep from jumping out the chair.

I looked up at him while I began bobbing my head up and down. I continued sucking until it was time I did that magic on him. I went all the way down until I covered his dick completely. I twirled my tongue around, and he really began to go crazy. He grabbed my head confused, not knowing if he wanted to push me back or hold me down. See, Mr. Fox's dick was bigger than our Dean's, Mr. Redland.

Mr. Redland's dick was fat, but it was short. What turned me off most about him was, his hands were short and fat, like his dick. He, himself, was short and stubby, and he smelled like mildew every time he lifted his shirt up. However, he was my meal ticket through school, so I satisfied him and sent him home to his wife.

Now, Mr. Fox, on the other hand, was sexy as hell and always smelled good. The difference was, Mr. Redland kept his feelings in his pockets, while Mr. Fox showed every sign of emotion. Every girl in school crushed on him but me. He was a simple fuck, and he kept the A's coming. Mr. Fox and I had more of a sexual bond until I sent him home to his wife, who was actually one of the counselors on campus.

I know what y'all thinking: this girl crazy. And y'all damn

right I'm crazy, but I wasn't born this way. I learned this shit from my uncle, Ray, who molested me starting at thirteen years old. Afterwards, he would always give me money and tell me, *"Use what you got to get what you want."* He would also add that I had a gift of magic, so y'all know what that was.

For years, he made me think what he was doing was right, until my aunt, his sister, caught him making me suck his dick. My mother went crazy, along with my father, and when I saw my mother cry, I knew the shit was bad. They hauled his ass off to jail, and seven years later, he was still there. My family cut him off, and my father, now a cop, was gonna make sure he spent the rest of his life behind bars.

Let me introduce myself before I move along. My name is Bambi Davenport. I'm twenty years old, and I spend my entire life on GSU campus. Back at my crib in Tampa, it was pretty boring because I didn't have the excitement in the hood like most. My mother worked as a social worker, and my father was a cop for Florida PD. When I say I literally have to walk around on pins and needles around them. I mean, I can't even have a phone. When I go to visit, I have to leave my phone in the car so they don't pry in my personal life.

Any who, as you guys know, I'm in college, and yes, I have a boyfriend. Zachery "Baby Bro" Vandiver. The finest nigga in school, and the star football player. Of course, y'all know how I snagged him; my magic trick behind the bleachers on the field, and that was exactly how I kept his cocky ass.

I stand at five-seven, and I weigh 142. I don't have all the curves and big asses y'all used to reading about, but I am pretty. Well, at least that's what everyone tells me. Also, y'all know I strip, and I work at one of the hottest clubs in ATL.

I'mma tell y'all like this: hold on to your seats because this is gonna go pretty fast. You're gonna laugh at my story, and you may even cry a little, but overall, you'll enjoy it (wink).

"Damn, you, girl!" Mr. Fox's soul left his body, and his chair went flying across the room.

I walked over to the trash can and spit out all the cum he pumped into my mouth. See, that's one thing I never did: swallow. They say big girls swallow, little girls spit. Well, give me a Barbie and two pigtails because I wasn't swallowing the shit. I mean, I have before, but I had to halfway like you. Mr. Fox hated when I spit it out, but I didn't give a fuck.

I wiped my mouth and retrieved my bag. I walked out of his classroom seductively because I knew he was still gasping for air. When I made it to the door, I turned to look at him. He was giving me that same desirable look he always gave me. I winked, followed by a smirk. I closed the door behind me and headed for my dorm. I needed to get some rest before my boyfriend started calling. It was Thursday night, so more than likely, we were going to one of our wild campus parties.

CHAPTER TWO

BAMBI

Boom! Boom! Boom! Boom!

I jumped up out of my sleep to the sound of someone banging on my door. I let out a deep sigh because I was in a good, deep sleep, dreaming about pizza. I loved me some pizza, and a bitch was starving. I sluggishly walked to the door, and when I snatched it open, ready to curse somebody out, Zachery stood there with a cold mean mug. Oh, Lord, here we go. I knew this nigga was about to start tripping.

"You don't see me fucking calling you?" He pushed past me and walked into my dorm.

"How when I was asleep? Damn, a bitch can't get no sleep?" I slammed the door.

I headed back into my room, and he was already sitting on the bed. I climbed back into my bed and slid under the cover. I was going back to sleep whether he liked it or not.

"Man, you need to get up. The party starts at nine."

"It's only seven."

"I know, but I need to swing by the crib and get some weed from Zone," he referred to his brother who was three years older than him.

I had never met him personally, but he was all Zac talked about. It was like he was obsessed with him. I mean, I understood he looked up to him or whatever, but everything he had or everywhere he went, it was, "my brother."

See, Zachery was spoiled as hell, which was why he always threw bitch fits. This Zone nigga had his head fucked up. I mean, my parents were well off, but Zachery had shit made. He drove a 2021 Camaro, and he even had a 2019 Range Rover. He was laced with VVS diamonds, and his wardrobe was so stacked—I never saw him in the same thing twice. Not to mention he was the star quarterback, and he even had his nickname, Baby Bro, on the back of his jersey.

The entire world called him Baby Bro, but I called him Zachery. He was a damn baby boy in a big girl's world, with his possessive ass. That was another thing; he was so gone over me it was scary. If I blinked wrong, he swore I was looking at another nigga.

"Yo ass tired because of that stupid ass job of yours," he retorted.

He hated that I was a stripper, but I used the fact that he met me as one to keep getting by.

"Why does it always gotta be about my job? Nigga, you met me as a stripper, so what's the problem now?"

"Ain't really a problem. You just put that shit before me," he replied, sounding dumb as hell.

I rolled my eyes and looked at him like he was crazy. I swear for him to be so cute he had a ugly soul. He was rude and cocky, and I was sure that came from him being spoiled. Zachery was a little on the light side, and he reminded me of Evan Ross. Yes, the little brother on *ATL*. The only difference was his sexy ass body he had built from playing sports.

"Whatever." I threw the cover off me and got up.

I knew it was over for my sleep, so I was just gonna get dressed. I headed to my closet and grabbed the first thing I saw, which was a pink dress that I was gonna throw on with a pair of Jordans because I definitely didn't feel like heels tonight.

"Hurry yo ass up," he shot and lay back on my bed.

I went into the restroom and began to run my shower. I knew this was gonna be a long night, so I couldn't wait to get some liquor in my system.

***

As me and Zachery headed out of my door, he grabbed my hand, and we made our way to his car. Just as we neared the parking lot, Mr. Fox was heading to his car and looked over at us. Our eyes met, and he gave me this weird look I couldn't read.

I hurried to turn my head, and when I did, Zachery was staring dead at me. Instead of him saying some slick shit like he normally did, he brushed it off and climbed into the car.

Often, I would complain about Mr. Fox to keep the heat off myself because once before, he asked me what was up with us. He claimed he saw the way Mr. Fox looked at me as if he wanted to fuck me. I made up a lie about me threatening him because he failed me. Of course, I overexerted my lie by asking him to beat his ass. When he said he would call his big brother, I had to stop him. Zachery always told me these wild stories about how dangerous his brother was, and I couldn't get Mr. Fox caught up.

To play things off, I looked at Mr. Fox again and flicked him off. Zachery began laughing, but Mr. Fox didn't find shit funny.

"Leave that nigga alone before he fail yo' ass again, Bambi."

"Fuck him." I playfully rolled my eyes and put on my seatbelt.

We pulled out of the lot and headed for Zachery's family's home.

***

When we pulled up to the home, of course, Zachery made me wait inside the car. He climbed out and ran over to an exotic car. The car was so beautiful. It gleamed under the sun, nearly blinding me because of how shiny the paint was.

Within minutes, Zachery came back holding a plastic baggy with the weed. He tossed it on my lap and climbed in the car. He made a U-turn just as the exotic car passed us by.

The driver looked inside, then nodded his head at Zac. I couldn't see his face, but his diamonds stood out, and his hat was turned to the back.

"Was that him?" I asked, assuming he was the brother Zac constantly bragged about.

He nodded his head yes and started the car.

"Where's your mom?"

"Shit, prolly out shopping. That's all she does." He shrugged it off as nothing.

I ain't trip, just like I never did because meeting mothers was personal. I had no intentions on being with him forever, so meeting his moms was pointless. Don't get me wrong, I loved Zac. I just saw no future for us.

Zac and I had been dating a little over a year, and seven months ago, we made shit official. He saw the way niggas acted around me, and because I would always remind him that I basically single, he decided to cuff a bitch, and I think he called himself throwing away the key. I didn't plan on being with him forever because he had a lot of growing up to do.

Truthfully, all these niggas needed to grow up. In my eyes, men were out for one thing, and that was sex. They all had a motive, and until a nigga swept me off my feet, I was gonna continue to be the dog bitch I was.

CHAPTER THREE

BAMBI

The next morning, Zac and I opened our eyes, and it was the same shit. He complained about his head spinning and wanted the trash can near the side of the bed. I didn't understand why this nigga drank like he could hang because he'd be man down for two days every time.

"Arrrrrgggh. My head..."

"Take the BC powder, Zac."

"You know I don't want that...arrrrrgggh." His head dashed for the trashcan.

I had to jump back so he didn't get vomit on my shoes. I shook my head and headed into the kitchen so I could make him something. He hated taking medicine because he said it made him vomit, so I was gonna mix it into a Ginger Ale.

"Morning, B."

I turned around, and Giovanna was standing there wrapped in a towel and bonnet.

"Hey, babes. Long night for you too, huh?"

"Hell yeah. I went to the Sig party in the Bungalows. They

shit was wild."

"I heard about that party."

"Y'all should have come. What's up with Zac? Nigga sick again?" she asked as she headed over to the Keurig machine to make a cup of coffee.

"Girl, yes," I replied, and she shook her head.

"I just don't understand why he thinks he can keep up with you. Bitch, you drink like a nigga. Hell, he can't even keep up with me, and I'm an amateur."

We both laughed because she was telling the real.

"Y'all can't fuck with the big dog!" I boasted.

"Bitch, them pills be having yo' ass drink like a fish." She rolled her eyes, laughing.

Again, she wasn't lying. I popped ecstasy pills whenever I went out because not only would it make me loosen up, but I could drink all night and wouldn't wake up like this nigga. I loved the way ecstasy made me feel, especially when I was in the club.

Believe it or not, I was a bit shy and timid as fuck. The owner of the Club Lorenzo was the one who gave me my first pill. The night I auditioned, he told me I was good. I knew how to swallow a dick whole, but I was too damn embarrassed to do it.

The next night, he made me come into work, and again, I almost punked out. He slid me the pill and told me it would help me relax. Nigga failed to mention it was a drug, and I would become addicted to the feeling.

"Damn, right, and I should have slipped his ass one." I rolled my eyes because Zac was screaming my name like he was dying.

When I walked back in, I gave him the soda and took a seat beside him.

His phone began ringing, but the nigga didn't budge.

"Zac, it's your brother." I handed him the phone, knowing he'd answer.

No matter how sick he was, or deep inside my pussy, the nigga would stop what he was doing to answer.

"Hello?" He moaned into the phone, extra the fuck out.

Again, I shook my head because the nigga was too damn

extra.

"The fuck wrong with you?" I heard his brother ask him through the phone.

"Hangover."

"Told yo' little ass stop drinking. You can't hang, my nigga."

"Fuck you."

"Yeah, a'ight." His brother laughed. "Check it, though. What day is your game?"

"It's Saturday."

"A'ight. We gon' pull up, but we gotta roll and catch a flight."

"A flight? You going wit' Mama?"

"Hell nah. Where she going?"

"She going to New York." Zac began choking, so he pulled the trash can in front of him.

"Nah, we heading to Cali."

"Oh, a'ight."

"A'ight, well, you get yo' self together, nigga. I'll see you Saturday." He disconnected the line, and Zac dropped his phone.

He lay back on the bed and began moaning like he was about to pass out.

I let out a small sigh and lay beside him. I had another two hours before class, so I was gonna spend some time trying to make this nigga better.

***

The Next Day

"You are something else, Ms. Davenport."

"I get that a lot." I smirked as I whipped my mouth and stood to my feet. I began fixing my blouse and let my hair down from the bun I had wrapped it in.

"From who? That little knucklehead boyfriend of yours?"

"From all you niggas." I grinned as I headed for the door. Just as I went to turn the knob, the dean called out to me.

"Ms. Davenport—"

"Don't tell a soul about this," I finished his statement.

He nodded once, and I headed out the door. I swear this nigga said this every time I sucked him off—as if I was gonna go around the school broadcasting what the fuck I did.

Little did the dean know, it was shameful even mentioning his name. It wasn't one of those situations like with Mr. Fox. Every girl on campus would die to be in my shoes. Now Mr. Redland was a different story. He was creepy as hell, and the entire campus talked about his bad body odor.

The moment I stepped into the hall, my eyes grew wide because Zac was coming down the hall with his backpack over his shoulder. He was looking dead at me, and I instantly became nervous.

"Hey, baby." I smiled as I hugged him because I was too scared he'd smell dick on my breath.

"What's up? What you here for?"

"Had to talk to dean about my tuition."

"Oh, okay. Nigga on some bullshit talking about suspending me from playing because I'm failing one of my classes." Zac shook his head, and this piqued my interest.

I knew the dean had to be picking on him because of me, and if that was the case, I was gonna holla at him the next time I came to see him.

"Okay, well, you handle that. I'm going to class," I lied.

My first stop was to my dorm so I could brush my teeth and change into something comfortable.

Zac and I dismissed each other and promised to hook up this afternoon. Because tomorrow was their big game, I was gonna see him at practice, then head to the club to work a night shift.

It was Friday night, and we had some ball players from Miami coming in. I knew it was gonna be raining money, and I damn sure ain't wanna miss out.

When I made it to the dorm, I could hear the radio on full blast, so I knew exactly what this meant: Giovanna was entertaining her man. I used my key to unlock the door, and sure enough, they were in the living room turnt up like it wasn't two-thirty in the afternoon.

The entire room was dark from the blackout curtains. Beyoncé's "Naughty Girl" was bumping loudly, and Giovanna was kneeled down in front of her boyfriend, Jayon, giving him a sexy strip dance. I swear this girl thought she was Beyoncé the way she was swinging her hair.

I hated to disturb her, so I quietly ran past them and into my bedroom. I couldn't help but bop my head to the song because I loved some Bee.

After changing into something more comfortable, I went into the bathroom to brush my teeth and rinse with mouthwash. Once I was done, I changed and headed back out the door to give the two love birds some privacy.

I made sure to grab my bag for the club later because I knew by the time I left Zac's practice, it would be time for work.

CHAPTER FOUR

WARREN "WARZONE" VANDIVER

"It's time for me to roll, shorty."

"But, why? You just got here."

"Man, don't question me, please. You know we ain't on that type of time." I slid into my shoes, and Tiara smacked her lips.

"But, Zone, you ain't even break me off."

"I ain't tryna be smelling like pussy in the streets. I'll prolly come back later."

"Yeah, we gon' see." She rolled her eyes, knowing there was no telling when she'd see me again.

The only reason I came was because I was in her neighborhood, and her raggedy ass friend, Hazel, told her she saw my whip. I swear the bitch always reported when she saw me in this part of town, but I bet the bitch ain't reporting how she sucked my dick in the Burger King drive-thru.

It never failed when it came to Hazel. She would tell Tiara if I had a bitch with me, but again, the bitch ain't tell her she wanted my dick to herself.

I walked out Tiara's crib and headed for my whip. When

I climbed in, I hit my nigga, Doobie, to see if them niggas were ready.

"Where y'all at?"

"We at the spot. You ready?"

"Yeah, I ain't tryna come all the way back over there because I'm by the school."

"A'ight. We bout to mount up now. Aye, y'all, let's roll," Doobie called out to the homies.

I disconnected the line and headed for my little brother's school. Today was their last playoff game to see who would go to the championship. I knew my little nigga was hype because he lived football. I swear the shit was his life. When Zac graduated high school, I made a pact with him that if he went to college, I was gonna cop him anything he wanted.

The little nigga chose money.

I blessed him with a hunnit bands, and our next bargain was if he played sports, he could get whatever. He picked a car, so I handed him the pink slips to two. I'd do anything for my little bro as long as he made a nigga proud.

Growing up, I didn't have a chance to do the shit Zac was doing. My diploma came from prison, and my college education was considered milestones. I spent my entire teenage years locked up all the way until I turned twenty-two. I was bounded over to an adult and was finally released three years ago.

I made a vow to myself that I wouldn't go back, and they'd have to kill me before they locked me in a cell again. Therefore, I made sure to move through these streets with caution. At only twenty-five, I lived a wild ass life, but because I ran shit in my hood, I wasn't one of them niggas who answered to nobody.

You couldn't put a burner in my hand and make me go do some dumb shit. I left that to the young niggas who ain't have shit to lose.

Although I ain't have no kids, a bitch, or none of that shit, I still had my moms and little brother to live for. Not to mention, I already had put them through enough. My entire bid, my moms

18

made sure to visit me faithfully. Most times, she would bring Zac, and each time, he'd cry for me to come home with them. When I got back to my cell, the shit would break a nigga down every time.

Just as I pulled up to Zac's school, my phone rang, and when I saw it was Yameka, I cursed myself because I totally forgot about her. Instead of answering, I let the call go to voicemail. I knew she was gonna chew my ass out because I forgot to pick her up. She even came to a lot of Zac's games when I couldn't make them.

Yameka was the closest thing I had to a girl. However, I wouldn't commit to her because I just wasn't ready. She was close to my moms and my little brother and has been for years.

Yameka was one of the three chicks who held me down while I was locked up. During that time, she built a bond with my moms and was damn near like family. She would be over there even when I wasn't present.

The shit irked me at times because it made me uncomfortable with bringing bitches around. Yameka wasn't having it, and my moms damn sure wasn't going for it. I really ain't give a fuck how she felt but, I still gave her some respect.

After sitting in the lot for about thirty minutes, a line of whips pulled into the lot, and Doobie was leading the pack. I counted seven cars as everyone parked, and I couldn't do shit but laugh. These niggas was some straight horndogs and was prowling on these college hoes.

Everyone came and surrounded my whip to wait for me to get out. We headed into the school and made our way straight to the field. When we walked in, it was like the entire bleachers turned to look at us.

Coach Carr looked up and saw me; he nodded his head and smiled.

I lifted my fist and nodded back.

Coach Carr fucked with me in a major way because of how

I looked out for the team. I helped fund their events and even bought their jerseys. In exchange, he let Zac put his nickname on his, which was Baby Bro. He had adopted the name since a kid, and the shit stuck with him until this day.

"Brooooo!"

I looked down to the field, and he was calling me, standing with his wide receiver, Nick.

"Just win, Baby!" I yelled back, and it hyped them up.

Before running off to the field, Baby Bro ran over and kissed a chick on the forehead. I watched as she smiled and stood to her feet. The game wasn't even started and already, she was clapping and whistling.

Brushing her off as one of his little groupies, I focused in on the game. I never paid Baby Bro's chicks no attention. Little nigga was the star on campus, and all these chicks wanted his ass. With the way we laced him and kept him in the latest whips, he was sure to have these hoes eating at the palm of his hands.

By the time the game ended, Baby Bro's team won by two touchdowns and a field goal. They did they shit, and I hoped like hell they could pull off the championship game. They were playing the Jaguars, and they were good as fuck. I swear if these niggas lost, I wouldn't hear the end of it. Zac was a real bitch when it came to losing, and he has been like that since he was a kid.

Me and my niggas headed down to the field so I could say my goodbyes. First, I slapped hands with Coach, then made my way to my little brother.

"Nigga, you saw that touch down!" he boasted the moment I was in his reach.

"Yeah, you did yo' shit." I rubbed the top of his head because he hated when I did that shit.

However, he was so excited he ain't trip. Instead, he was smiling hard and dapped up a few of my niggas.

"I gotta catch this flight, so we 'bout to roll."

"A'ight be safe."

"Always," I replied and went to turn around.

Before I could walk away, Baby Bro's little chick ran over to him and jumped into his arms. Again, this shocked me because the only thing he loved was football. I watched the chick for a brief moment while sizing her up.

She was pretty as a muthafucka with a small frame. The way she was dressed made her seem like she was out of his league. When she looked at me, she began staring like she was wondering who the fuck I was. She was eyeballing a nigga so hard she didn't even hear Baby Bro talking to her.

"Let's roll," I told my niggas, and we headed off to our whips.

I had a plane to catch, so I needed to get some shit in order. I was only gonna be gone for three days because I was meeting with a new connect who was taking over my old connect's empire.

***

"Yooo," I answered the phone for Pablo, who was the new connect.

"Zone, there's been a change of plans. We're coming in."

"Word? I was on my way too. That's even better."

"We land at about six a.m. I'll call you with a location."

"A'ight, fasho."

I disconnected the line, glad I didn't have to deal with the airport. I looked over to Doobie, knowing he'd be happy because the nigga hated them long ass flights just as much as I did.

"Change of plans. They coming down."

"Hell yeah!" The nigga was excited. "I'm 'bout to go get some pussy. Drop me off to my whip."

"Nigga, just be up at six."

"Damn, they landing early. A'ight."

I jumped over to the left lane so I could bust a U and head for my mom's crib to take Doobie to his whip. Making it back in no time, we pulled up on her block. There were a million cars out front, and the sound of loud music could be heard a mile away.

"Somebody got it popping," Doobie said, watching the many cars. This wasn't typical for this area. It was always so quiet because no one lived here but older, retired families.

"Nigga, I know I ain't tripping." He lifted from his seat when he realized the party that was cracking was in my mom's yard.

My mom was out of town, and she damn sure wouldn't be having no wild parties.

"I know this nigga ain't..." I frowned, noticing all the college kids hovering around the yard.

I shook my head as I climbed out my whip because this nigga, Baby Bro, dun' lost his everlasting mind.

"Everybody, get the fuck out my yard! Go home!" I yelled out to the few people who lingered around.

I stormed into the house to find Baby Bro, and when I say this nigga had it lit? It looked like some wild college shit. Bitches was wilding, niggas was screaming, and everybody was drunk as fuck.

I walked over to the DJ booth and snatched his shit out the wall so hard his speaker flew. Everyone stopped to look at me, but no one moved. I pulled my strap from my waist and cocked my shit.

"Everybody get the fuck out before it be some bodies sprawled out in this bitch!"

The entire room scattered, knowing I wasn't playing. I then stormed off to find Baby Bro, and the nigga was ducked off in the backyard by the pool. The chick from earlier was sitting on a pool chair, and Baby Bro was talking to a few dudes.

"Nigga, have you lost yo' fucking mind!"

He looked up at me with a scared look. "Come on, Zone. Moms out of town," he slurred, drunk as a skunk.

I shook my head because the nigga knew he couldn't handle the shit.

"Nigga, in my mama crib?" I questioned, because he knew I ain't play that shit when it came to her crib.

Hell, she would flip out if she knew this nigga was on some dumb shit.

"Man, everybody get the fuck out, and I ain't gon' say it twice!"

Baby Bro looked down at my strap, but the nigga was too damn drunk to realize what was going on.

"Get yo' dumb ass in the house." I slapped him across his head, and he stumbled. "Little mama, you gotta roll," I told the chick who had been by his side all day.

She looked from me to Baby Bro and stood to her feet unsurely. She was now dressed in a little ass dress that barely covered her ass. Her hair was in a high ponytail that hung long. I was able to get a really good look at her, and the little bitch was pretty as fuck. I couldn't front, my little brother scored with her, but right now, I ain't care about all that.

"Ummm...uhhh, I came with Zac," she spoke with a little head roll. Her eyes were glossy as hell, and she, too, looked drunk.

"Where you stay on campus?" I asked, and she nodded.

"I'mma drop you off because that nigga ain't driving nowhere like that." I shook my head, looking at Baby Bro. "Man, go lay the fuck down." I jumped at him, ready to knock his drunk ass into the pool. I walked away from him before I did something I would regret.

He wasn't in his right mind, and I wanted to beat his ass sober.

Once I made sure the house was cleared out and Baby Bro was tucked away in his room, I locked up and headed out the door. When I got outside, Doobie was sitting in his whip, and the chick was standing there.

I hit the alarm to unlock the door, and she climbed in. I headed over to Doobie's whip to remind his ass to be up early. After we shot the shit for a few minutes, I went to my car so I could drop ol' girl off.

As we drove towards the campus, ol' girl was in my passenger seat feeling herself. She was snapping her fingers and dancing in her seat to every song that came on. I was still a bit upset, but I wasn't gonna kill her mood. After all, it wasn't her fault her little nigga was gon' get his ass beat.

From time to time, I would catch her watching me, and she had this look on her face like she was checking me out. I tried hard to ignore her ass, but she was making shit hard.

"What's up? Why the fuck you keep looking at me like that?" I asked so she would know how obvious she was.

"I don't know. I guess because you cute." She shrugged boldly.

Shit took me by surprise because I damn sure ain't expect her to say no shit like that.

"Shorty, you drunk."

"I ain't drunk. And if I was, so? I can handle my liquor," she sassed.

"Girl, shut yo' young ass up." I chuckled.

"Young? I ain't young. I'm a grown ass woman."

"Yeah, okay." I laughed again and continued to drive.

The car got quiet except for the music that was playing until...she slid over closer to me and put her hand on my lap.

"The fuck you doing?" I asked, looking at her like she was crazy.

"Showing you how grown I am," she replied and unzipped my pants.

A part of me wanted to stop her, but I wanted to see how far she would go. That was the dumbest shit ever because her bold ass pulled my dick out and wasted no time wrapping her lips around it.

She began teasing the tip until she got my shit wet. I continued to drive until I felt her entire mouth go down and cover my whole dick. I wasn't no little dick nigga, so most definitely, this bitch was grown.

Scurrrr!

I lost control for a second and damn near wrecked my shit.

"Hold up, shorty." I pulled over to the side of the road.

She didn't even bother stopping. She began swallowing my

dick like a damn vacuum, making me damn near jump out my seat.

I couldn't help but grab her head as my face frowned. I didn't know what the fuck this chick was doing, but she damn sure sucked a lot of dick in her life. Not even ten minutes, and I busted the fattest nut. This shit was a world record.

When she came up, she had a smirk on her face and not a drop on her mouth. She swallowed my kids with no effort.

I looked over at her with my face still balled up because this bitch was vicious. *I don't know where Baby Bro got her from, but he needs to take her back*, I thought as I shook my head and pulled off.

Yeah, I didn't know what the fuck just happened, but the shit happened that fast. I prayed like hell he wasn't in love with this girl because like I said, she was out of his league. She was gonna have my little brother gone, if he wasn't already.

CHAPTER FIVE

BAMBI

One week later

"**S**o are you going to the game tonight?"

"I don't know. I may have to work."

"Girl, Zac would die if you missed the biggest game of the year."

"I know. Maybe I'll go to work after."

"Okay, well, my man is waiting on me back at the dorm. I'll see you tonight." Gio ran off to meet with her boy toy.

It was time for me to head to Mr. Fox's class, so I made my way down the hall for Latham Hall. When I made it to the class, Mr. Fox was already in the middle of his lecture. He looked up and titled his head to the side. He gave me that same look he always gave me as if I knew better. Of course he had to say some slick shit.

"Well, it's nice of you to finally join us." He didn't look pleased.

I knew this had to be because I had been dodging him and

his class. This entire week, I had been working at the club, so I was tired as fuck. It's not like he was gonna fail me anyway, so I really didn't give a fuck.

"I'm here now." I sat my book down, annoyed.

When the class was over, I tried to hurry and rush out, but Mr. Fox called my name. I stopped to turn around, and again, I showed him I was annoyed.

"So where have you been?" He rubbed my arm and licked his lips. Mr. Fox knew he was fine as fuck.

"Mr. Fox, are you falling in love with me?" I smirked at his annoying ass.

He looked at me, and surprisingly, he didn't say some slick shit. Instead, he looked at me with fire in his eyes. "What if I—" Before he could finish, he was interrupted.

"Fredrick."

We both turned around, and Mrs. Fox was standing in the door.

"Just make sure you have it done by next Friday. This project is important," he tried to play it off.

I pursed my lips and threw my bag over my shoulder. I walked out of the room and made sure to roll my eyes at his wife. She always looked at me dirty like I wanted her nigga. Yes, I was sucking Mr. Fox up—even fucked him a few times. But I ain't want his ass. Real shit, I ain't want none of these niggas.

Everything was a motive for me because it's what I was taught. *"Use what you got to get what yo' ass want."*

Right now, I ain't want no real relationships. The one I had with Zac was childish, and I had a feeling it wouldn't last too long. I couldn't believe we actually went nearly eight months together. However, if it ever got out about his brother, he would damn sure stop fucking with me.

Keep it real, I really ain't care, and I would do it again. It wasn't out of spite; I was just that type of chick. I really didn't have feelings for niggas because I tucked them away in my pockets.

Him and his brother could get fucked. Truthfully, now that I had encountered the great Warzone, I'd prefer him. Not only was he holding major dough, but he had so much dick he could make a bitch bowlegged.

I didn't know if Zac and Zone had the same father, but them niggas not only had two total different dick sizes, they looked completely opposite. Zac was light-skinned, and Warzone was a beautiful ass chocolate nigga.

His entire demeanor screamed drug lord, and he had a smile so impeccable he'd make any girl melt. His waves were like currents in the Pacific's shore, and from the way his white-tee hugged his arms, he had a body to die for.

Now that was the only resemblance he and Zac had; they both had nice bodies. I'm not saying Zac was ugly. He just wasn't fucking with Zone.

After changing my clothing and pinning my hair up, I checked my phone to see if Zac had called. I knew he wouldn't because today was a big day for him.

"Hey, you coming to the game?" I stuck my head into Giovanna's room as I walked by.

"Yeah, let me slide my shoes on." She jumped off her bed and slid into her shoes.

After grabbing our bags, we headed out to the field.

After the five minute walk, Giovanna and I made it to the game, and it was already lit. We flashed our school badges and were let in by security. When we got on the field, the lights were bright, and it was now night. We found us some seats, and the moment I sat down, I spotted both Mr. Fox and Mr. Redland. It was like, right on cue, they both looked over at me, and I flicked them both off secretly.

Giovanna awkwardly looked at me and began laughing.

"Yo ass is crazy." Gio continued to laugh.

"Mr. Fox a bitch ass nigga. He's trying to fail me," I lied.

Mr. Fox would never fail me because he wanted that magic

throat.

"I seriously doubt that. I think he has a thing for you."

"He's married."

"That doesn't mean shit. The other day, he asked if I saw you. He tried to say something about a project that was coming up, but I ain't buy that shit. He looked too damn desperate."

"I don't think so," I replied and got quiet.

Just as the game was gonna begin, the entire bleachers full of patrons stopped to look at the entourage of niggas that had walked in and demanded everyone's attention.

The first one I spotted was Zone because, of course, he led the pack. They all took their seats, and for some reason, I watched him in awe. He was rocking a pair of grey sweats, a white crisp tee, and some Air Force Ones. I couldn't help but shake my head because the nigga had on a grey fur coat that looked lot it cost a fortune. Although the outfit sounded hideous, only a nigga like Zone could pull it off.

Assuming he felt someone watching him, he turned to look in my direction. Our eyes met, and we held each other's gaze for a short period of time. I quickly turned my head to let him know I wasn't pressed by him, and when I glanced back, he nodded his head with a chuckle.

Giovanna looked over to Zone, then over to me curiously.

"Who's that? One of your boo's?" she asked because she knew I had a flock of niggas.

Although G wasn't a close friend of mine, she was my dawg and dorm mate. She also knew Zac didn't hold my interest enough to only entertain him.

"That's Zac's brother."

"Oh," she replied and looked onto the field.

Just as we looked down, her boo was scoring a touchdown. We jumped from our seats and began cheering. Every now and then, I would steal glances over at Zone, and each time, my pussy would jump between my legs. Suddenly, a light-skinned Keisha chick, with a long weave, walked over to where they all sat and took a seat next to him. *Hoe ass nigga. Girl, I had his dick all down my throat,* I thought while watching them, then I turned my head unbothered.

Nearly an hour later, there were seven minutes left in the game, and The Cougars were down by twenty-one. In the football world, seven minutes was a long time and enough to make three touchdowns. However, Zac and them were playing like they had already given up. Well, not Zac because he was the only one still playing hard. He played so hard he actually scored.

"Go baby!" I screamed towards the field.

It was now down to five minutes, and things still weren't looking good. From where I sat, I could see the frustration on Zac's face. Gio was still cheering them on, but the outcome, if they lost, would rain down on me. Her and her nigga were gonna go off like two love birds, while Zac talked shit, cried, bickered, and distance himself.

Now I was mad I called off work because I damn sure ain't wanna be around him like this.

CHAPTER SIX

WARZONE

It was the last minute of the game, and I knew the shit was over, so me and my niggas stood to our feet to head down the field. The Cougars lost by one touchdown, so the entire yard was moping. I knew Baby Bro was gonna be bugging, so I needed to holla at him to let him know he had done a good job.

As I hopped down every bleacher, I couldn't help but look over at Bambi, whose name I discovered from my bro. Every time, I stole glances at her, she was watching a nigga. Yameka was with me and right by my side, and the way Bambi was acting, I knew she thought this was my bitch. Yameka was the only chick with me and my crew, and it didn't make shit no better she was under me.

When we walked onto the field, Baby Bro was shaking his head. I could tell the nigga had already shed a couple tears, and any minute now, it looked like he would break down. I called his name, and first, he acted like he wasn't gonna come, then he snapped back to his senses. He walked over to me with his helmet in his hand, and just as I was about to speak, Bambi walked over with another chick.

"You gon' do this bitch shit in front yo' chick?" I whispered to him, and he looked over in her direction. "Man, straighten yo' fucking face, dawg. You keep forgetting you can't carry the whole team. Nigga, you did yo' shit, you hear me?"

He nodded his head yes.

"You go get cleaned up. We going up at my crib for you tonight. I got a surprise for you too." I patted him on his shoulder and walked away from him.

No matter what, my lil' bro was the shit on that field, and win or lose, couldn't nobody take that from him. Because of that, I made sure to give him some fly shit to let him know. Baby Bro loved gifts, and me being me, I kept my word.

I motioned for the homies so we could roll, but before I walked off, I looked back because I could feel Bambi's eyes watching me. We held each other's gaze for a short period, but I broke that shit because shorty was on some wild shit. Baby Bro was standing right beside her, although he was in another world.

Every since that night she sucked a nigga up, I had been feeling guilty every time I talked to him. I didn't think she meant shit to him until now when I noticed she was at every game. The night I dropped her off, he woke me up in the wee hours asking did she make it home, and that's when I knew he half-ass liked her.

In my eyes, Bambi wasn't shit but a dick gobbling skeeza, but a nigga couldn't front. Every since that night, all I could think about was the way she swallowed my whole dick. A part of me was hoping she would be here tonight, just to see her lips.

Last night, I got some head from Yameka, and I shook my head the whole time thinking 'bout Bambi. I swear I was good on her ass, and I was gonna make it my business to stay away from her. I knew tonight Baby Bro would end up drunk, but fuck that. Her ass was going back in a Uber, a helicopter, a pedal boat, or something. All I know was, she wasn't getting in my whip.

***

"Keisha? (Kei), Jasmine? (Jas), Kiera? Megan? (Go)
Lisa? Ashley? (Ashley), Sierra? Sarah?
She got her hands on her knees with her ass in the air
Ooh, that lil' bitch a player..."

I walked through my crib watching how all the little college chicks twerked their ass to Megan and Da Baby's "Cry Baby" song. I swear these little hoes were ratchet as hell, and I wondered if they parents knew what they ass be up to on campus. I didn't invite the whole damn school like Baby Bro did at my mom's crib, but it was enough of them to turn up the entire den.

My den was big as fuck with a bar, arcades, and all kinds of other shit to do. I was barely home, but when I was, this was the room I'd chill in and watch sports.

Baby Bro was looking a little better, especially after I handed him the keys to an updated Mustang. The whip was a 2021 with a fire red paint job and red rims to match. The nigga was so excited he looked like he wanted to cry from that. I swear my little nigga was a fucking cry baby, and he ain't give a fuck.

"Aye, bro, let me crack this bottle." Baby Bro held up a bottle of 1738.

I looked from him to the bottle, and as bad as I wanted to say no, I couldn't.

"Man, go ahead. I swear yo' ass throw up in my crib, I'm beating yo' ass drunk or not." I walked out of the room. I was trying my best to let them party without being uncomfortable.

"Yo, little throat baby out there." Doobie pointed behind him as he entered the crib.

"Man, fuck you. That's that man's throat baby." I chuckled and shook my head.

This nigga always had jokes to crack about that night. It made me regret telling his ass. However, I couldn't help it. Bambi's head was so fire. I had to tell somebody.

"What's up, Zone?"

I turned to look at her when I heard her voice. "Sup." I nodded my head and looked the other way.

She continued on to the back, and I couldn't help but watch her. She was changed into a pair of little ass pussy-cutting shorts that were so short her hair came past them.

"On my mama, I want a sample of that." Doobie watched her with his hand on his chin, sizing her up. "You think Baby Bro in love with that bitch?" he asked seriously.

"Man, leave that man's chick alone."

"Hell nah. Not the way she got yo' ass. I need a bar, Zone." He continued to watch her until she disappeared into the den.

"She ain't got me like shit. Fuck you." I brushed his stupid ass off, knowing I was lying.

I was happy Yameka was here tonight because ain't no telling what the fuck my ass might do. Like I said, I was trying to avoid shorty, and that was exactly why I had Meka here.

Four hours later, I had finally made my way into my bedroom. Everyone was still downstairs, but a few people had left. Yameka and I had come up about an hour ago, and she was now asleep, mad.

I tried hard to fuck Meka, but for some reason, my dick wasn't getting hard. She tried to suck my shit the best she could, but she couldn't get me right for shit. She took her drunk ass to sleep, so I laid here smoking a blunt. A part of me wanted to go downstairs and be nosey, but I ain't wanna look like a weirdo.

Doobie was gone to our trap, so wasn't nobody downstairs I could really fuck with it.

"The fuck?" I mumbled, looking over towards the door.

The silhouette of a woman stood there, and by the curves, I could tell it was Bambi. I watched her as she walked into my room, not even bothering to care that Yameka was lying across my bed. She walked over to my bed as she watched for my reaction.

Once again, she was on some bold shit, and I wanted to see how far she would go. She stood over me, then looked to Yameka, who was still knocked out. She then bent down and landed on her knees. She motioned for me to scoot closer to the edge, so I did it carefully so that I wouldn't wake Yameka. Since I was only in my briefs, all I had to do was slide my dick over the top, but I was gonna let her do that. *This bitch just don't give a fuck*, I thought. Because she did just that. I wondered if she even thought about Baby Bro right downstairs, who was prolly pissy drunk throwing up all over a nigga house.

Wasting no time, Bambi wrapped her juicy ass lips around my dick and began going to work. She made sure to suck me whole but keep the bed steady. She began sucking the life out my dick with no hands, damn near making me wanna cum already. It was crazy how Yameka couldn't get my dick hard, but here comes Bambi, and my shit stood at attention.

I swear I ain't even have to purposely choke her with my dick like I did most bitches because she was already swallowing it with no effort. She was sucking, slurping, and every time she spit on it, it was like my dick grew harder. At this point, I didn't give a fuck if Yameka woke up. This shit felt too damn good, and wasn't shit gonna stop me from busting a fat nut down Bambi's throat.

CHAPTER SEVEN

BAMBI

A Week Later

"**B**ambi, yo're on next. Yo' ass been missing in action. These niggas been here looking for you."

"You act like you forgot I'm in college."

"What the hell that got to do with me? You think I can't replace you?"

"No." I rolled my eyes at Lorenzo, the owner of the club. "Lo, these bitches can't do it like me, and you know it. You can try, but you won't ever find a bitch like me."

I stood to my feet in my six-inch stilettos and strutted out of the dressing room, leaving Lo stuck. He had me all the way fucked up with his threats. He could try to replace me all he wanted, but no bitch in the city could walk in my shoes. I held the crown in this bitch, and if he thought these old, washed up bitches could do better, he thought wrong.

I've worked here a year, and in such a short time, I racked up more than all these bitches in the few years they had been here. Don't get me wrong. Club Erotic had some bad bitches who were stacked. However, the things I could do on that stage was unheard of.

I didn't have much ass, nor did I have one of them paid-for bodies, but I was perfect. Keep it real, an ass couldn't compare to these lips. My segment of the show alone was what brought the niggas here; he could play if he wanted to.

When the DJ announced my name, the entire club went into an uproar. From where I stood, I could see Lo, so I hit him with a wink. The nigga had this dumb ass look on his face, but he only stood there to watch me. I let the crowd go crazy until they calmed down, then I made my entrance. I was gonna make magic happen in this bitch tonight, just like any other night.

I did a sexy walk to the edge of the stage, then bent over for them to kiss my ass. Literally. I then flipped over to the pole and landed in the splits. I used the pole to pull me up and climbed all the way to the top. While I was up there, I scanned the crowd of people with a cocky demeanor, then twirled all the way down, landing into the splits again. And just like that: money shower. Crazy part was, I was just warming up. I had another twenty-five minutes, and I was just getting started.

***

By the time I made it to campus, I was tired as hell and only had about five hours before my first class. By the time I took my shower and fixed something to eat, I would only have about three and a half, so I knew I would be sleeping in class.

I stepped out of my ride and hit the alarm. The moment I made it onto the pavement, I could feel someone in the near watching me. It was three in the morning, and Zac had already gone to bed. Too afraid to turn around, I walked fast as fuck towards my building.

"Bambi."

My name was called, and boy, that voice sent a chill through my body. I slowly spun around because I had to be dreaming. *Hell nah, I ain't dreaming.*

Zone and I locked eyes. He was leaning on his car coolly with his hands slightly in his front pockets.

"Zone," I called his name, not believing it was him.

He walked over to me and stood right in front of me.

"Wha...what." I had to clear my throat. "What are you doing here?"

"I'm looking for Baby Bro."

"Oh, ummm...did you call him?"

"Yeah, nigga ain't answering."

"Well, last time I talked to him, he said he was going to sleep."

"Oh, a'ight," he replied, but he didn't move.

No words were exchanged, and the only sound around us were the crickets that lurked in the trees. The moment was awkward as hell, so I chose to speak.

"I'm gonna go. I'm sleepy as hell."

"Where you coming from? One of yo' little nigga's house? It's three in the morning, shorty. You shouldn't be outside this late."

"No, I wasn't at one of my nigga's house. They all sleep," I taunted, and he chuckled. "I'm coming from work."

"Word? Where you work at?"

"Sharkys," I lied, and I didn't know why.

Sharkys was a bar that sold beer and pizza. Every Tuesday, people from campus would go for Taco Tuesday. Some days I would join, but most days, I had to work.

"Oh, okay. That's what's up. Well, you have a good night. Make sure you tell Baby Bro I was looking for him." He turned around before I could reply.

I couldn't help but watch him until he made it to his car.

I let out a deep sigh because a part of me wanted to tell him to come into my dorm and fuck me. However, I decided against it because I know he was already thinking I was some crazy wild bitch. Sucking him up while his girlfriend lay on the side of him, was a bit over the edge. But, hey. He let me.

The dose of magic I gave Zone was all he would get. The only nigga I fucked was Zac because to me, sex was personal. The only person I've fucked, other than Zac, was Professor Fox, and that only happened twice. It was the biggest mistake ever, and since that day, I refused to give him some pussy. I was sure that's why he was acting weird, which was why I couldn't do it again.

When I made it into my dorm, I kicked my shoes off and headed into the kitchen. I began searching for something to eat but only came up with a microwave burrito. I grabbed a 7UP and headed for my room. The moment I sat down, I tore into my burrito and even burned my tongue a few times. I was starving.

Once I was done, I lay across my bed, too tired to shower. I couldn't help but let my mind wonder, and it drifted to Zone. It was weird how he showed up to my dorm for Zac when he could have went to his. No matter what, Zac would always answer his door. The even crazier part was, how did he know where my dorm was located?

Brushing him off, I closed my eyes and tried hard to go to sleep. Just as I felt my eyes getting heavy, I heard a soft knock at the door that made my eyes flange open. The eager part of me quickly jumped to my feet. I headed for the door, and I didn't know why, but I was nervous.

I let out a sigh before opening it, and when I flung it open, Zone was standing there with his head cocked to the side. He bit into his lip, and Lord, my panties got wet as fuck. Apparently, he was here for something other than Zac, so I opened the door for him to enter.

My heart began to flutter as I closed the door behind him. Apparently, he figured my room was mine because he entered without an invite. I followed behind him, and when he locked the door, this nigga told me he really wasn't here for Zac.

He then walked over to me and rubbed his fingers into the crouch of my shorts. A soft moan escaped my lips, and my body grew with fire at just his touch.

"Take this shit off, ma," he demanded, looking me in the eyes.

I watched him for a moment, contemplating my next move. Just ten minutes ago, I vowed to myself that I wouldn't have sex with him, and here I was, ready to let him bang my back out. I stepped out my shorts, and he began to undress. *Damn*, I thought when he came completely out of his clothing because his body was made from perfection.

"Come here, ma." He motioned for me as he stroked himself.

I walked over to him, and my damn heart wouldn't stop beating through my chest. He reached down into his pocket and grabbed a condom. His shorts fell to the floor, followed by his briefs, and for some reason, his dick looked bigger than every time I've sucked it.

"Bend that shit over, Bambi." Again, he demanded in a raspy voice like he meant business.

Using his hand to help, he bent me over the dresser and wasted no time spreading my cheeks. He slid inside of me, and thanks to the condom, we had lubricant. My body got tense because this man felt as if he were gonna come out through the roof of my mouth.

He started off with nice, slow strokes, and when he found his rhythm, he began to hit it hard.

"Ahhhhhh....shhhhhhittt...ooohhhhh...shitttt!" I cried out because this nigga was killing me.

His dick felt like it was growing by the minute, and he knocked the wind out of me.

"Nahhh, big bad ass. Where you going?" He pulled at my long weave, then wrapped it into his hands.

He continued to pound inside of me, ignoring my cries, but the shit was turning me on more. I took a deep breath and relaxed. I began to slowly throw it back, and it must've turned him on because he began pulverizing my pussy harder than before. He lay his body on my back and whispered into my ear.

"For you to be so bold, you sure can't take no dick. Bambi, I don't know who you be playing with me, but, ma, I ain't one of these young niggas. I will murder this little pussy and send yo' ass to the ER."

I swear I didn't have a comeback. However, I was happy he stopped stroking because he was too busy talking shit.

Zone turned my body around, then forced me to look at him. When I didn't reply, his face softened a little, but I could tell he wanted to continue waxing my shit. Instead, he pulled me to the bed and pulled my covers back. He motioned for me to get into the bed, then he followed behind me.

He climbed in and turned me to my side. He wrapped his arms around me, then lifted my leg. As he slid into me from behind, he never disconnected his embrace. He began stroking in and out of me, but this time, he was going slow.

I didn't know what the fuck he was doing to my body, but my pussy began cumming repeatedly. This time, I was moaning softly with a more gentle satisfaction. His dick felt so good. I had to admit to myself no nigga had ever gave me no dick like this. However, I wasn't gonna tell him that.

I was gonna keep the same energy because this nigga had me fucked up. I had a reputation I had to live up to, and a nigga like Zone wasn't gonna knock me off my square.

Or so I thought.

CHAPTER EIGHT

BAMBI

A couple hours later, my eyes flung open to the sound of my bedroom door. I looked over to the side of me for Zone, but he was gone. I was so tired I never heard him leave.

After hours of fucking, he finally caught his nut, and we just lay there. He held me in his arms until I dozed off, and I couldn't lie. It felt like I belonged there.

"Bam!" I heard Zac call my name, so I became nervous.

Damn, did he see him leave? Does he know?

My mind began playing tricks on me. When he called my name again, I got up to open the door because clearly, he wasn't going away.

"The fuck you doing? You didn't hear me knocking?"

"I was asleep," I replied annoyed, turning to head back over to my bed. I plopped down, and suddenly, my eyes landed on the empty condom wrapper. *Oh, shit!* I thought as Zac took a seat on the opposite side of the bed.

"So you not going to class?"

"I'm tired."

"Why? You went to work last night?" he asked, knowing damn well he didn't wanna hear the truth.

"Yes," I replied, and he nodded. I could tell he had some slick shit to say, but he kept it to himself. "Why aren't you in class?" I quickly changed the subject.

"Shit, I came to lay with you. I ain't got class until two forty-five with Ms. Hendrix." He took his shoes off.

Again, I became nervous, not knowing if my bed smelled like sex. When he pulled the cover back and got in my bed, I was waiting on him to say it. Instead, he slid close to me, and when his hand brushed up my leg, I knew exactly what he wanted: some pussy.

"I'm not in the mood, Zac. I'm sleepy as hell." I moved his hand.

Although his dick wasn't that big, I couldn't dare fuck him. My pussy was still throbbing, and I hadn't even taken a shower. All I wanted was him to leave so I could go back to sleep.

"Your brother came by looking for you."

"Who, Zone?" he asked as if he had a million brothers.

"Yes. That's your brother right?"

"Why he ain't come to my dorm?"

"I don't know. He said he called you."

"Oh, a'ight. I'll hit him," he replied and turned to his side.

I was happy as hell because that meant he was going to sleep. The moment I heard light snoring, I was gonna get the empty condom wrapper.

***

"Most prokaryotes carry a small amount of genetic material in the form of a single molecule, or chromosome, of circular DNA."

"I'm so damn tired of Prokaryotes."

"What was that, Bambi?"

"I said, I'm tired of Prokaryotes, Mr. Fox. We've been going over this same damn lecture for weeks. We get it. The DNA in prokaryotes is contained in a central area of the cell called the nucleoid, which is not surrounded by a nuclear membrane." As soon as I said it, the entire class laughed, making Mr. Fox upset.

"Just for that, you're staying after class to write a SA on the subject, smart ass."

Yeah, I bet you do want me to stay after class. I thought, wanting to say it out loud so bad. Instead, I smirked because I knew this was coming.

After the lecture, everyone excused themselves, so I remained seated. I pulled out a piece of paper to pretend I was really gonna write a dumb ass SA.

Mr. Fox waited for the class to clear before he made his move. He walked over to my desk and stood in front of me. He watched me as if I were being punished, but I could see the desire in his eyes. When he dropped to his knees, it blew me back because he had never done no shit like this.

He wasted no time sliding his hands up my dress and pulled my panties down. He took one of my legs out and cocked my legs open. From time to time, he would look at me, but I kept my game face on. I knew he was contemplating what he was about to do, but again, that desire was eating away at him.

Mr. Fox dove into my pussy, face first, blowing me back. He began devouring my pussy like a starving child, making me open my legs wider. One leg hung in the air, and the other now rested on the chair beside us. He began ticking my clit with his tongue, and when he found that spot, he stopped right there. I mean, letting out slight moans, and I pushed his head further into my pussy.

"Right there...Oooh, shit, right there."

I practically had the nigga in a head lock. No wonder why Mrs. Fox was head over heels. This nigga had some fire ass head. He continued to chew at my clit, and I continued to moan. This nigga's head was through the roof—I couldn't hold back. My body became hot and had the sudden urge to pee.

"Ahhhhhhh!" I let out a grewsome scream, and a gush of liquid shot out of me like a damn tidal wave.

My clit instantly became sensitive, so I pushed his head back. I jumped to my feet and looked down at him. His face was covered in my juices, and he didn't seem to mind. I shook my head at the nigga and slid my dress down.

"I'll see you soon, Mr. Fox."

I grabbed my bag and tossed it over my shoulder. I headed out the door without bothering to look back. I walked down the hall so fast because I needed to get away from his class. My body was hot, and I could barely catch my breath.

When I made it outside the, breezy air felt good as hell against my face. I sighed, feeling refreshed, then got a grip on myself. I had never in my life nutted like that, and I knew exactly why. The whole time he was eating my pussy, I imagined it was Zone.

Lord, I didn't know what the hell this nigga was doing to me, but I didn't like it. I wanted thoughts of Zone out of my head, but it seemed like his face was everywhere. It was like I could still smell his Bond No. 9 cologne lingering in the air. I had to wash my damn sheets to get rid of his smell, but oddly, I could still smell it.

It had been a week since he left me, and it seemed like Zac was around more. Everything he did was starting to irritate me. I finally gave him some pussy, and it was like I began to compare him to his brother. I tried to fuck him in the same spot I fucked Zone, but it didn't work. He just wasn't giving me that satisfaction Zone had giving me.

Yesterday, he asked me to roll with him to his mother's house, but I declined. I dodged that bullet, but I didn't know how long that would last because his birthday was coming up, and he asked me to join him on a trip to Maui.

It was our two-week spring break, so I agreed to go. I knew Zone wouldn't be coming because he was street nigga. His lifestyle came with a twenty-four/eight hustle, so I knew he wouldn't have the time.

CHAPTER NINE

WARZONE

"**B**oy, get yo' hands out my damn pot. The food is for our guest."

"Damn, I'm hungry, Ma."

"Well, wait until Bambi gets here." My mom grabbed the pot of cooked noodles from the stove and dumped the water from them.

I paused when I heard Bambi's name. "What she coming over for?"

"Because she's your brother's girlfriend. Why, did you meet her?"

"Yeah, I met her." *And she had my dick way down her throat,* I thought after replying.

"Oh, okay. Well, she's staying the night. We have a flight in the morning."

"Where y'all going?"

"Hawaii."

"Damn, why y'all never ask me if I wanna roll?"

"Because you're always too damn busy. And anyway, it's Zac's birthday. Their on spring break. You're welcome to come along."

"Hell yeah, I wanna go." I smirked, but she didn't even know why. "Well, Yameka is coming to."

"Never mind, Ma." I shook my head.

"Don't be like that. I'm sure she won't get in your way. You can have your own room."

"I'm definitely getting my own shit," I replied, thinking 'bout Bambi.

Since the morning I left her crib, it seemed like that was all a nigga could do. I thought the bitch had some fire ass head. That girl had pussy to match. It was crazy how attracted I was to her, and I think that was because she didn't come with attachments.

Like falling in love.

Bambi was savage as fuck because she wasn't like these other hoes. They were clingy and wanted time that I couldn't give them. I ran a lucrative drug empire, and that's where all my time and attention went to. However, for this trip, I was gonna make time.

I knew with Yameka tagging along, and Zac being there, it was gonna be hard to fuck with Bambi, but if I could at least see her, I was cool with that.

"I'll be back."

I grabbed a piece of fried chicken off the tray before she had a chance to object. I shoved it into my mouth and headed for the door. Just as I was walking out, Yameka walked in carrying a duffle bag, a small travel bag, and was pulling a suitcase.

"Damn, you ain't gon' help me?"

"My bad, ma." I grabbed her shit and took it to the living room.

"Where you going? Yo' mom cooked. You ain't staying?"

"I'm 'bout to run home and pack."

"Pack?" she asked curiously.

"Yeah. Shit, I'm going to Hawaii too."

"Oh, okay," she replied, and I could see the excitement in

her eyes, but I shut her down.

"I don't know why you looking like that. I'm 'bout to snatch me a little island bitch, and you bet not hate." I smirked and headed for the door.

"You got me fucked up!" she shot over her shoulder, but I ignored her.

Yeah, I was gonna get me an island bitch alright. Bambi.

***

"I flushed my feelings down the toilet 'cause you shitted on me
I fucked up, you got a nigga and stop waitin' on me
We ain't together but I know you still got feelings for me
And last night I text your phone and told you, 'Put it on me...'"

In mid route, my phone rang, and it was Doobie. I hated when my phone rang when I was in a zone vibing to my music. I was off this Vory "Ain't it Funny." His whole album was dope, and I ain't really care for new rappers. These days, the music wasn't what I fucked with because I was a young nigga wit' a old soul. I listened to Jay-Z and Jeezy.

"What, nigga?"

"Man, fuck yo' music. Fuck you at?"

"'Bout to go pack. Moms taking us to Hawaii."

"*Taking* us? Nigga, you prolly paying fa the shit. But how you rolling out without me?"

"Yo' ass ain't gotta come everywhere, nigga."

"Man, fuck you. Who all going?"

"We are going for Baby Bro's b-day. Him and his chick."

"You mean, yo' chick?" Doobie chuckled. "Baby Bro gon' beat yo' ass when he catch y'all. I think the little nigga could take you."

"Fuck you. I'll beat you and Baby Bro's ass. I ain't even on shit with shorty." 43

"Bullshitttt. My nigga, you stalking the bitch, all at her college campus."

"You know what, bitch? I'm 'bout to hang up."

"Nahhhh, nahh, I'm just fucking with you. Check it, we at Blue Flame. Waffle Mamazzz out here. She got the city lit."

Waffle Mamazzz was a food catering business that was based out of South LA. She cooked all types of shit, and the shit was fire. She catered events in the most upscale parts of Los Angeles, and all the hood niggas, dboys, and rich niggas fucked with her. Her instagram @_nocelebrity rang bells. She was a hood chick out of Watts wit' a cold grill game.

"I'm 'bout to pull up."

I hung up before he could taunt me about Bambi. Lately, this nigga been having jokes. He wasn't used to me inquiring about no chick, so he was grasping the shit like I was. He was the only nigga who knew my every move because we shared locations. Therefore, he hit me the next day asking why I was at ol' girl campus in the wee hours of the morning. This was my nigga, so I couldn't lie. Anyway, he knew the full details off bat. So I couldn't lie if I wanted to.

After the short ride on Highway 85, I pulled up on Latijera Road. I looked for one of Doobie's whips and spotted his Burgundy G Wagon. Because there wasn't a park by him, I turned on the side street and pulled up to the corner. I hopped out and left my shit right in the street and still running. I strolled over to Doobie and the many chicks who stood around him. The streets were lit, and he wasn't lying. The whole city was out. I nodded my head to the few people who had enough balls to chant my name, but I never stopped. I ain't fuck with the public like that, but I kept shit cordial.

"Hey, Zone."

"'Sup, Jashell?" I spoke and walked past her.

She was a thirsty ass chick I'd smashed when I was fresh out. When I say her pussy was trash. It was a waste of a time and a pretty face. Jashell was bad as fuck, but with pussy like that, it was no wonder she ain't have a nigga.

"What's up, bro?" Doob chuckled and gave me a dap.

"Shit. I'm 'bout to get some food," I told him and walked over to the food truck. I put my order in and walked back over to Doob.

"Nigga, it's going up at Erotic next week. Zo having a twerk contest, and Yung Baby performing."

"Yeah, that shit gon' go up. I'mma fuck with you if I'm back."

"Man, yo' ass crazy. Why the fuck you going?"

"It's Baby Bro b-day."

"Nah, nigga. You going because Bam's ass going. You're starting to like her, huh?"

"Hell nah. It ain't shit like that."

"You gon' lie to me?" He turned to look at me seriously. "Exactly." He laughed and shook his head. "I say just tell the nigga it's a hostile takeover. You want his bitch, and he can't beat yo' ass."

I fell out laughing because this nigga was crazy. I wish it was that easy. Baby Bro was feeling Bambi. Not to mention, if I did have the chance, I'd prolly shake her in a week. I got bored with bitches fast, and although she was fine as fuck, I knew there had to be a flaw to her.

"I'mma figure something..." I went to say, but I stopped in my tracks. "Is that that nigga, PJ?"

Doobie looked in the direction I was looking. Before he could confirm it was him, I whipped out my strap because this nigga was dead today.

"Zone, not..." I heard Doobie say, but it was too late.

I was already up on the car. When the nigga looked up, his eyes grew wide as if he seen a ghost. He threw his hands up when he saw my strap.

Pop! Pop! Pop! Pop! Pop! Pop! Pop! Pop!
Pop! Pop! Pop! Pop! Pop! Pop! Pop! Pop!
Pop! Pop! Pop! Pop!

I let off every round into the car, killing him and the driver. Everyone around started screaming and ducking for cover, but the scene was over. I tucked my strap back into my waistband and jogged over to my whip. Doob did the same, so when I pulled off, he was right behind me. Instead of going home, we drove out to my boy, Hank's, welding company to get rid of the strap. When we pulled up, Doobie jumped out his whip, and I did the same.

"Nigga, I was tryna stop you because them cameras."

"Man, I wasn't even thinking. You already knew when I saw that nigga, it was on sight."

"I know, but bro, we got niggas to handle that. All them people were out there. Ain't no telling who gon' point yo' ass out."

"*Me?*" I pointed to myself, and he nodded.

He had to rethink his statement because no one in their right mind had the nuts to point me out. I really didn't understand why he was tripping in the first place. The nigga, PJ, I knocked down was really his beef.

Back when Doob was fresh out of prison and a corner boy, them niggas robbed him. I was still locked up, but I was released a month later. We ran into them niggas in traffic, and when Doob told me what happened, a war broke loose. I killed two of PJ's boys, but I was unsuccessful with him. After that, every time we saw them niggas, it was on sight. Finally, I handled the nigga, but I knew shit was about to get wild.

He had three brothers who were heavy in the streets, and I knew they were gonna come gunna for us. Typical hood shit in my city, so I was prepared. I had long money and plenty guns. Not to mention, I had a crew of raw niggas who bust they guns for fun.

CHAPTER TEN

BAMBI

"Why he gotta come?"

"What you mean? It's my b-day."

"Not like that, damn." I had to stop Zac because he was defensive. "I just don't think he likes me."

"Why would he not like you? You ain't did shit to him. Just stay out his way." Zac threw his duffle bag in the backseat, and I could tell I got under his skin.

I watched Zone as he hopped into the backseat of a Lincoln Town Car, along with his bitch and Mrs. Vandiver. Today was my first time meeting her, and she was hella cool. I've talked to her on the phone since the trip was planned, and we hit it off. A few times she mentioned Warren, so I assumed that was Zone. *Ugly name for a fine ass nigga,* I thought the moment she mentioned it. However, I didn't think he was tagging along.

I didn't plan on being all up under Zac, but I did want to relax. It's bad enough I had been thinking 'bout Zone on a regular basis. Now here he was, coming to Hawaii to shift my whole mood (sigh). I was ready to get this trip over with already.

"I can't wait to get out here and fuck with my boy, Muta." Zac brushed his waves, hyped.

"Who's that?"

"He played for The Cougars our first year. He had to move back home because his pops died. They got a football league out there. I'm 'bout to go run them niggas," he boasted as he continued to brush his hair.

I swear right now, he reminded me of Chicago from Poetic Justice brushing that weak ass fade. I looked at him like he was crazy because I now knew he had a purpose for this trip.

"So that's why you picked to go there?"

"Hell yeah. Why else?"

"Ummm...maybe to be romantic. I thought we were gonna enjoy each other on this trip, Zac."

"We can enjoy each other on campus. I ain't seen my boy in almost a year."

Wowwww, I thought, still looking at him like he was crazy. "Yeah, a'ight," I replied and turned to face the streets.

This nigga really fucked my mood up, and because Zone had his bitch with him, I knew the chances of saying fuck it and giving him some attention was over with. I sat back in my seat, mad. I could have stayed and went to work at the club. At least I'd be getting paid, and the men there didn't waste my time.

***

"Aloha 'oe i ko Hawai'i"

We were greeted the moment we stepped off the plane. We were helped out to the cars and were handed brochures of everything there was to do, including our hotel activities. After that long ride, all I wanted to do was shower. Everyone mentioned going out to eat, but I was gonna take a raincheck.

When our car pulled up to the hotel, I quickly climbed out because everyone was too damn friendly. I now see out here you have to be enjoying the atmosphere to enjoy the island. Because I was annoyed, I wasn't enjoying shit. I wanted to let Zac gone 'bout his business and get the fuck away from all of them.

"Bambi, you have your key?"

I turned around at the sound of Mrs. Vandiver's voice. "Yes." I nodded, trying hard to not let her know my energy was off.

She was excited about this trip, so I didn't want her to think I wasn't happy. Not to mention, I didn't pay for anything.

"Okay. Zac ran off, but we're gonna get dressed for dinner."

"Okay," I replied and stuck my key into the door.

I let out a breath of air because I needed this peace. I began to unpack my bags and pulled out my Alexa speaker so I could play some music. I went straight to my YouTube playlist and to my loving-making playlist.

"Two people, just meeting, barely touching each other
Two spirits, greeting, tryna carry each further
You are one, and I am another
We should be, one inside each other..."

Trina Broussard's "Inside My Love" began to play, and I moved around the room. When I noticed the nice-sized hot tub, I began running water with bubbles. After a few moments, it filled up, so I began to undress. Just as I was stepping out of my Ruthless Chicks sweats, there was a small knock at the door. Assuming it was Zac, I opened the door and made sure to peak outside before fully opening it.

"What's up?"

"Man, Bambi, you know what's up." Zone pushed past me and headed inside.

"Zone, I just want to relax," I told him with my heart racing.

For some reason, I was nervous as hell. Maybe because I knew Zac could come at any minute. This shit wasn't like back at the dorm because he wasn't confined to my dorm or bed. Here, it was different. This nigga and I shared rooms.

However, this was Zone. The nigga I was secretly lusting over no matter how much I told myself *stop. Just fucking stop.* The craving, the suspense, and the satisfaction of knowing how he put it down had me woozy.

"Man, Bam, you know what it is, ma. I'm 'bout to go shower, and I'll be back. Don't worry 'bout yo' little nigga. He busy footballing." Zone looked me in my face seriously. He walked back over to the door and turned to look at me before walking out. We having dinner at the 27th Hut. "Don't wear no panties." And just like that, he disappeared.

I closed the door upset, knowing he was already gone, but I didn't give a fuck. Ugh, this nigga had me fucked up. He always had me fucked up, and I didn't care how much I told myself that.

***

"Nice of you to join us, Bambi. Have a seat." Mrs. Vandiver smiled and pulled the seat back for me to sit on.

The moment I took my seat, Zone's little girlfriend mugged me. Zac nor Zone were seated with us because they both were still getting dressed, so I focused my attention on the ocean. Everything was so alluring. The lights from the fire torches gave the ocean a bright orange glare, and the breeze was perfect for the night. It was my first time coming to Hawaii, and everything was just as I pictured it. Tonight, we were just having dinner, but tomorrow night was Zac's birthday and some big extravaganza.

"Here comes these knuckleheads," Mrs. Vandiver stated, looking in the direction Zone and Zac were walking.

When they made it to us, Zac was smiling hard, and Zone instantly focused on the women. I shook my head because his bitch was sitting right here, and he didn't care. The chick rolled her eyes, and I couldn't help but chuckle. She shot me a fucked up look, and I smirked, pissing her off more. Already, she was giving me dirty looks, and I knew it was because Zone and I were obvious. We might not have been obvious to Zac, but that was because women weren't fools. We could tell when a nigga wanted to smash the next chick.

Keep shit real, I didn't think Zone really cared because he watched me every chance he could. Just like now. This nigga looked in my direction every chance he got. The looks he gave me weren't as if he wanted to know his brother's girlfriend. They were more of a, *damn, I'd fuck her, and fuck Zac.*

CHAPTER ELEVEN

WARZONE

The next morning, I opened my eyes to the sound of ocean waves, birds chirping, and an instrument that sounded off the entire island. I couldn't figure out what it was, but the shit had a radiant sound that echoed. When I rolled over to my side, Yameka was on the side of me asleep. She caught me last night drunk and came to my room.

When we first arrived, she was mad I didn't share rooms with her, but that was out. I was tryna get Bambi in this bitch so I could blow her back out. Keep it real, I'm mad she had even come. Last night, she made a statement about Bambi liking me, but I brushed it off as her just tripping. I could already see where this shit was going. Yameka was gonna get to prying in my mix. Not to mention, acting like she was my bitch. She was all over a nigga last night at dinner, and I sensed she did it to make Bambi mad.

However, I shitted on her because I cracked a bad little Hawaiian bitch. Even Bambi wasn't looking salty, but I did it because I wasn't feeling how she was all over Baby Bro. I mean, I understood that was his bitch, but fuck that. Bambi belonged to me. She ain't have to do that shit while a nigga was sitting here. Therefore, I played the game with her.

I climbed out the bed, and before going to handle my hygiene, I headed to the balcony. When I stepped out, the sun met me, and the air made a nigga take a whiff. Shit was really a breath of fresh air. I was glad I came. I spent so much time locked up I never really got a chance to explore different shit. Hawaii wasn't somewhere I would choose to come because it reminded me of some romantic shit, and I definitely wasn't no lover boy.

"Morning."

I turned around, and Yameka was standing in the doorway. "Morning," I spoke back, then turned back to look at the ocean.

She took it upon herself to join me, but she didn't interrupt my thoughts. We both looked out into the air, but of course, this would only last a few minutes. I knew Meka all too well, and her ass was contemplating something.

"You know, Warren. I was thinking we should just take the next step."

I knew it.

"Mek, we've had this talk a million times. I'm not ready for that."

"And why? Because you wanna be a hoe."

"Yeah...I mean, not just that, but yes. I been gone so many years of my life a nigga ain't ready to be tied down."

"Am I not pretty enough?" she asked, dropping her head.

I looked at her like she was crazy because Meka was beautiful. She had one of those cute, sassy ghetto girl looks, but she was innocent. Meka was a real woman, and one day, she was gonna make a nigga a happy husband. It's just not me. The way she held shit down in my family without being my bitch, I could only imagine. I never had to worry about niggas or her name ringing in the hood. Meka was dope as a friend, but something always told me if I were to ever be with her, shit would go left.

"Meka, you pretty as fuck, ma. I'm just scared I'll hurt you. The day I decide to get into a relationship, I don't wanna play games. We too strong for me to tear you down. Right about now, I'll only hurt you, and that's what I'm not trying to do."

She looked at me, and I could tell my response was not what she wanted to hear. "One day, I'm gonna find a man to love me, Zone, and you're gonna regret it," she replied and headed back into the room.

I didn't bother looking at her, but that statement did kinda put something on my mind. I knew the shit was real, but really, I ain't give a fuck. I didn't want a bitch, and couldn't one, not even my mother, force that upon me.

***

It was the night of Baby Bro's official birthday, so we were going out to the island to turn up. I had rented an entire section of tee-pee's, had them decorated, and paid a few Hula dancers to turn Baby Bro the fuckup. One thing about me, I turnt up no matter where the fuck I was at, and I made sure to go big when I did.

One of the dancers being Lydia, whose number I got last night, was instructed to give Baby Bro a show. Afterwards, I was gonna bring her back to the room for a one night stand and a private show. I mean, what were the odds of me coming back out here and seeing her again? Slim to none.

When I walked up to our table, the first person I noticed was Bambi. I raised my eyebrows in awe because she was looking sexy as fuck. She wore a coconut bra, a grass skirt, and even a flower in her hair. She blended right in with the foreigners of the island. A part of me got jealous just knowing that Baby Bro was getting some birthday pussy from her. This drew me ahead to look over at Meka, who sat next to moms. I guess she ain't get the memo. However, she was looking sexy too in an all-white flowy dress. Her hair was in a long ponytail, and her jewelry was simple.

It amazed me how Bambi adapted with the culture, and this only told me a chick like her knew how to have fun.

"Hakimo! Let the party begin!" I whistled to the guy who helped me orchestrate the evening, and he knew what I meant.

He rushed over to the bar and began scrambling around to bring us drinks. I looked at Baby Bro, and he was grinning wide, knowing how I got down. Tonight, he was gonna definitely get fucked up and possibly throw up, like always.

"Baby Bro, you ready to throw up?" I chuckled, and he flicked me off.

"Bet a hunnit I ain't throwing up tonight?"

"Bet five hunnit to your one?" I pulled my money out and tossed it on the table.

"Oh, leave that poor boy alone." My mama laughed, taunting his little ass.

"Nah, Ma, yo' son think he can fuck with the big dogs. It's just a friendly bet. As a matter of fact, we gon' start the first round off with shots."

Just as I said it, Hakimo sent one of the Hawaiian chicks over with a platter of shots. I looked at Baby Bro and winked. Everyone grabbed their glass, and on the count of three, we all threw back our shots. I called out for another round because we were just getting warmed up.

"Bambi, so where do you work?" my mother asked Bambi, and I could tell she caught her off guard.

"Mom, can we not do the fed game with all the questions?" Baby Bro chimed in, and it was something about the nervousness on his face that grabbed my attention.

"It's okay, babe. I work at Sharkys. It's a bar that serves only beer and pizza.

"Oh, okay. Sounds fun."

"It is. And the tips are really good." Bambi smiled and grabbed another shot from the tray. She looked at me, so I grabbed another one.

Everyone else followed and grabbed their shots. Once we took them, Hakimo brought over another platter with coconuts drinks and a Mai Tai, which was my mother's favorite. We all began to chat until our conversations were cut short by the show that was gonna begin.

The loud beat of the drums roared across the island, and it snagged everyone's attention. The Hula dancers began to come out one by one until they formed a line. The lights began to change colors, and a large fire pit grew from the ground. All the dancers circled around the pit and began moving their bodies to the beat. One dancer in particular walked over and grabbed Bambi by the hand. She then pulled her over to the circle, and to my surprise, Bambi wasn't shy. The lady began showing her the dance, and Bambi caught on quickly.

I threw another shot back and sat back to watch the show. As beautiful as the women were, my eyes were set on one: Bambi. I watched how her body moved forcefully to the beat. Our eyes connected, and she didn't break our stare-down.

Baby Bro stood to his feet, and already, I could tell he was faded. He walked over to where Bambi and the dancers were, and they all surrounded him. Two dancers in particular began dancing on him, and Bam didn't seem to mind. Instead, she began dancing on the drummer, and by the smile on his face, he found her attractive.

I stood to my feet and grabbed my cup. I walked over to join my brother and made sure to pass him another drink. Nigga drank it with ease, forgetting all about our bet. He was so in tune with the women I think the nigga even forgot his bitch was not too far away. He was on some drunk shit and began groping the women, overly enjoying himself.

"Nigga, you forgot yo' girl was right there?" I leaned over to whisper.

"Man, fuck her. You don't see these bitches? They all bad," he slurred.

I shook my head and that told me right there he ain't appreciate a dope chick. In my eyes, Bam was dope as fuck, and tonight, she proved just that. Not to mention, she was just as beautiful as the women out here, but this nigga chose to fuck up his life for one night.

From time to time, I could see the frown on Bam's face every time she looked in his direction. Meka wasn't making shit no better because her drunk ass kept screaming, "That's right, bro!"

Suddenly, I turned around, and three women surrounded me. I couldn't help but dance back. Again, I looked over to Bambi, and she wasn't pleased at all by our behavior. I got so in tune with the women I never saw her run off until my mother began to call my brother's name. When I looked up, I caught the flow of Bambi's grass skirt running across the sand. She was going in the opposite direction of our rooms and into the dark.

"Ma, can't you see I'm busy?" Baby Bro blew my moms off.

I shook my head and contemplated running behind her. It was dark as hell, and we damn sure ain't know shit about these people or this island.

"I got her, Ma," I told my mother, and she thanked me. Little did she know, she ain't have to. In my eyes, Bambi was my bitch, so I was going to get my bitch.

I began power walking in the direction I saw Bambi run, but I didn't see her in plain sight. I began power walking in the direction I saw Bambi run, but I didn't see her in plain sight. I continued to search for her, and when I found her, she was sitting in the sand. I walked over to her, knowing I was gonna get my shoes wet, but for this moment, I ain't give a fuck.

"Leave me alone, Zone." She sounded frustrated but didn't look at me.

"Man, you trippin. That little nigga just having fun," I tried to justify for him.

Just watching the frown on her face made her little mean ass look sexy. It was dark, but the glow from the moon shined down on her face and titties. My dick grew hard every time the wave crashed against her thighs, and this only made me crave her more. Taking it upon myself, I grabbed her hand and pulled her up. I pulled her right into my arms, and to my surprise, I kissed her. I then bent down to place kisses on her breasts and made a trail down to her stomach. She let out a soft moan and tilted her head back, inviting me in. Hungrily, I pulled one of her breasts from the coconut bra and began sucking it.

"Zone. Stop, please. Someone..."

"Shhhhh," I told her and lay her body back into the sand.

This time because she was completely lying down, the water flowed through her hair and slightly splashed on her face and body. I lifted the grass skirt and pulled her panties off. I stuck them into my pocket, and that was when it hit me. I didn't have a rubber. Damn.

A nigga was so damn horny I didn't let shit stop me. I released my dick from my shorts and put it to her opening. I made her wrap her legs around me as I slid into her slowly. Because of the mood and setting, I was gonna take my time with her. I began slowly stroking her, and she was still trying to run.

"Ahhhhh, shit!" she screamed and her voice echoed into the air. "Zone, its hurting," she cried out.

"Take it, baby." I growled into her ear.

I continued to stroke her, and we were both now soaking wet. Between the ocean water and the wetness from her pussy, I didn't know which was wetter. Her pussy gripped my dick each time I went in and out, and each time, she said my name.

"Bam, I keep telling you this my pussy. On my mama, you bet not fuck that little nigga while we're here." I thrusted into her hard, meaning exactly what I said.

"Okayyyy," she continued to cry out, sounding sexy and innocent.

"I'm not playing, ma. This shit mines." I began kissing on her neck.

I could tell she didn't want me to kiss her, but she had me fucked up. I forced her lips into mine, and she finally gave in. She began kissing me with force, like she had been waiting for this moment.

"Zone, ohhh, shit...I'm cumming...ohhh, baby! I'm cum-min..."

That was all I needed to hear. I started hitting her pussy fast, with long strokes. Each time I came out of her, I rubbed the tip of my dick against her clit. That shit had her so gone—she let out a loud scream and came all over my dick. I kept coaching myself to pull out, but her pussy felt too damn good. I couldn't.

"Can I cum in my pussy?" I asked, not giving a fuck if she said no.

"Ohh, yesss," she whimpered softly in a seductive tone.

I could tell she was still cumming—if not, cumming a second time. This only made matters worse. I couldn't control the nut that was beginning to ooze out. I spilled it all inside of her until I ain't have shit left. Her body began shaking, and she tried hard to catch her breath.

"Zone, I love you."

I stopped in mid-stride to look her in the eyes. I was trying to read her because this shit took me by surprise. "Don't say that shit if you don't mean it, ma."

Again, I surprised myself by my reply. Nah, I wasn't gonna say it back. Whether I felt love for her or not. I knew it was the heat of the moment that made her say it. Tomorrow, she was gonna be ignoring a nigga texts and be laid up with Baby Bro.

"I do mean it. I love you, and I'm sorry."

This time, her cry was different. I knew that any moment, she would have tears in her eyes.

"Ain't shit to be sorry about. You feel how you feel, ma."

"That's all you got to say?" She pushed me up and lifted up from the sand.

I slid my dick back into my shorts and fixed myself.

We were still sitting in the sand, and shit had now become awkward.

"What I'm supposed to say? Like, be fucking for real. I love you back? That's what you wanna hear?" I looked at her, but she remained quiet. "Bam, how the fuck I'mma love a bitch that's about to go lay up with my bro? Yes, a nigga got feelings for you. Yes, I want you in the worst way, but you belong to that little nigga." I fumed, and I could tell I hurt her by my choice of words.

"What if I leave him?" she asked, and I didn't know what to say.

I mean, what could I say? I wasn't a relationship type nigga, and if, so how the fuck would it work? Bambi belonged to Baby Bro.

"You ain't gone do that. And anyway, I ain't looking for a girlfriend. We fuck, and that's what it is."

She looked at me with so much hurt in her eyes.

I turned my head, not being able to face her. Out the side of my eye, I saw her stand to her feet.

She looked down at me and was still watching me. "So that's just it? Just a fuck?" she asked, and her voice cracked.

When I didn't say a word, she shook her head and ran off. I dropped my head because a nigga ain't want shit to go like this. I didn't expect this conversation, and especially now.

I sat right here in this same spot and got lost in my thoughts. I tried to imagine life with Bambi as my girl. Then the thoughts of hurting Baby Bro played in my mind, and I began to imagine how left shit could go if he found out. I knew I would hear it from my mother, and definitely, this shit would kill Meka.

Was Bambi worth all that, was the question. Truthfully, I prolly would never find out. I was already in the wrong, so asking her to leave him would be fucked up. A nigga lived his life heartless, but I had a conscious. At this point, I knew me and Bambi were prolly done, and I was fine with that. Shit, I avoided love because reality was, I prolly could have fallen in love with her. She was dope in my eyes, but the fact still remained that she belonged to my muthafucking brother.

CHAPTER TWELVE

BAMBI

Boy, when the tables turn, they spin. Just a week ago, I was masking my feelings for Zone, and now, here I was confessing my love for him. I let the liquor get the best of me, but like they say, a drunk speaks a sober mind. I also knew it had something to do with the way that man fucked me on the sand right in the ocean.

Now I was delirious and looking dumb. I swear I was on some revenge shit. I wasn't a fool. Zone was digging my flava, but I couldn't really blame him. I did belong to Zac, and because of this, I was gonna show his ass.

"Morning. What time is it?"

I looked over at Zac, who had finally opened his eyes. Last night, like any other night, he passed out on me. Drunk. He ended up losing the bet because the nigga was throwing up like he had an exorcist.

"It's one p.m. How are you feeling?"

"One!" he jumped up. "Damn, I'm late for the game." He began scrambling around the room.

"Zac, the game doesn't start until four."

"I know, but we have to do warm ups," he spoke as if this were a championship game.

It wasn't shit but a street nigga game in the middle of the sand. I shook my head because since we've been here, we really hadn't vibed. Truthfully, I didn't give a fuck, especially after last night. I was still on some fuck him shit, but I needed him for my vindictiveness against Zone.

"Zone came looking for you. It looked urgent," I lied.

He quickly grabbed his phone and dialed his number. Perfect.

I crawled over the bed to where he was standing and pulled his dick from his briefs.

"What's up, nigga?" he asked Zone just as I wrapped my lips around his dick. "Ohhh, shit..." He moaned, forgetting he was on the phone.

I wasted no time putting his entire dick into my mouth and began tickling him underneath with my tongue. Again, he began to siss and moan. I began sucking his dick so good the nigga did exactly what I wanted and said my name. He pulled the phone from his mouth, but I was sure Zone heard him.

"Nigga, what the fuck you doing?"

"Shittt...man, you gon' make me cummm...fuck, Bambi..." Zac began panting like a bitch.

"Man, hit me back!" Zone yelled into the phone, and I could hear the frustration in his voice.

I smiled on the sly and made Zac bust with no control. He was still holding my hair for dear life as his dick shrunk inside my mouth. I pulled back and went into the restroom to brush my teeth. My job was done, and I was now back not fucking with him.

"You coming to the game?" He looked over and asked.

"Nope, tell yo' little Hawaiian bitches from last night to go." I rolled my eyes and began looking for something to wear for the evening.

"Wow, for real, Bambi?"

"For real, nigga. You disrespectful as fuck, so I'm good."

"You good on me?" He looked over as if his world was gonna end.

Anytime I threatened to leave him, he would die. I knew this was only because he ain't want the next nigga to reap the benefits of this throat. Zac ain't love me. The nigga only loved football, but he made sure to hold onto my ass.

"Yes, I'm good on you. When we get back, I'm going to work, and everything you were doing, I'm doing. Only difference is, I'mma do it better, hoe."

He stood there frozen because what could he really say? He knew he was wrong, so he ain't put up a fight. However, the look on his face told me I pushed a button. He already hated that club, so all I did was add injury to insult.

"I swear on my mama..." he went to say as he slid into his pants. He did this anytime he wanted to get far the fuck away from me.

Before I could laugh at his ass, my phone rang, and it was Lorenzo. A part of me didn't want to answer because I never answered when I was with Zac, but today was different.

"Hey, Zo."

"Bam, I have someone here who wants to talk to you."

"Who might that be?" I asked because it was too early in the day.

"Hold on," he replied, and I could hear him passing the phone.

"Hello, Bambi?"

"Yes?" I frowned, wondering who the hell it could be.

"Hey, Bambi, it's Cletus. When are you gonna come back to work? I miss spending my money on you, baby."

Again, I frowned, wondering why Zo was calling me for Cletus. Cletus was prolly the oldest nigga in the club, and Zo knew damn well how I felt about him. He wore a pair of bifocals, and he was scrawny as hell. He was one of my biggest tippers, and it was evident he was obsessed with me. Everyone knew in the club he was obsessed with me because he was always on some creep shit. Every dancer there tried hard to get Cletus, but he wouldn't budge. A few times, Zo tried to get me into the private room with him, but hell no. He was too damn creepy with bad breath.

"I'll be there tomorrow, Cle. I'm flying out today," I replied to him, and Zac shot me an evil glare. I turned to look away from him because I definitely wasn't trying to use Cletus as any get back.

Zac knew all about Cletus because I've mentioned the crazy things he always said and did in the club. To my surprise, we'd laugh about it, but today, he wasn't laughing.

"Okay, sugar. I'll be waiting on you."

"Okay."

I hung up the phone before Zo could say anything else. This nigga was dumb as hell for the call because he knew where I was at and who I was with. Lorenzo hated Zac because he felt I was out of his league. He would often bicker about Zac's age, and I would always remind him to stay out of my personal life.

"You can't wait to get back to that club." Zac shook his head.

"Damn right. I need my money." I pursed my lips and moved my head side to side.

Again, he shook his head and headed for the door. As soon as he left, I lifted from the bed and began moving around. I went to take a much-needed shower and was thankful I dodged the bullet.

My pussy was throbbing from Zone last night, so all I wanted to do was let the hot water run down on me. After, I was going down stairs to hop into the jacuzzi and relax. Our flight wasn't due to leave until later this evening, so I had plenty of time.

***

Home sweet muthafucking home, I thought as our plane landed. I was so happy to be home and getting away from Zac. The entire flight, he wore a pair of headphones and rapped the entire way. I didn't wanna be bothered with him, so I slept every chance I got.

When the captain said we could now depart the plane, I jumped to my feet and grabbed my luggage. I bumped right into Zone, and he mugged me, just as he did the entire way back. I grabbed my bag from the overhead and headed down the aisle. I decided to take an Uber back to my dorm because I definitely didn't wanna ride back with them.

"Bambi, where you going so fast? Our car is out front. We're gonna go to the house, and Warren is gonna take you to your dorm."

"I'm okay," I replied to Mrs. Vandiver. That was what she told me to address her as.

"Oh, okay. I mean, you don't have to, but if you insist." She shrugged.

I thanked her and smiled because I damn sure wasn't trying to ride with Zone. That nigga was really in his feelings about the stunt I pulled with Zac, but who gave a fuck? I was in my feelings too.

Just as I made my way out the door, my mother began ringing my phone, and a part of me didn't want to answer. I quickly answered, hoping it would be brief because I needed to contact Uber.

"Hey, Mommy."

"Bambi...hey, baby. How are you? How was your trip?"

"I'm great. We just landed. It was a great place to visit."

"Oh, that's nice. So are you coming home for a few days? I'm sure you don't have to go back to school soon?"

"Yes, Ma. I'll be there in a couple days."

"Okay, great. We'll send your plane information. Your father wants to talk to you as well."

"Okay, well, I'll be there."

"Okay, love. You take care, and we'll see you soon."

"Okay, Mother." I smiled and disconnected the phone.

I was excited to go see my parents, although it would be a game of 21 questions. My mother was the cool one; it was my father who was very militant. Especially because he was a cop

—he tripped out on everything. Now don't get me wrong, my mother was hella strict also. Her job as a social worker went to her head, and she always had these wild stories about taking people's kids.

"I'll see you when I get there."

I turned to look at Zac, who walked up on me, pulling his luggage.

"No the fuck you won't." I rolled my eyes.

He shook his head, and when I looked away, I locked eyes with Zone. We gazed at each other momentarily until I rolled my eyes at him too.

Moments later, my Uber pulled up, so I climbed in. I looked at my calendar, and I only had a few days until I went to my parents' house. This meant I would only work a few days, and Zo was gonna be mad. However, I needed to see my parents because it's been a minute. I was gonna make sure to pull a double shift, which would be announced my first day back. Like always, I was gonna pack each shift out because my tippers were dedicated.

MF: *I really miss you.*

I looked down at the text. It was from Mr. Fox, so I ignored it. I dropped my phone into my bag and sat back for the ride. At this point, I just wanted to bury myself in my bedroom and escape the world. Everyone could suck my ass right now, and I meant that disrespectfully.

CHAPTER THIRTEEN

BAMBI

"We dealing with a love cycle
When we first met, I shot her with a rifle
I'm a thug, so it's hard to wife her
Stamp like a brick, so you don't need a title..."

"Ladies and Gents, she's been gone for a minute, but she's back to give you something electrifying. Fellas, get yo' dollas out for mt girl BAMBIII!"

I emerged to the dance floor and began seducing the crowd immediately. I walked to the head of the stage wearing a Grim Reaper gown, and underneath, I wore a black leather G-string two-piece. I wasn't taking off anything until the money started flying. Therefore, I wound my hips and locked eyes with the men I knew were here to pay. I was also using this time for the song to change. Because we had a birthday in the club, I decided to play...

"Birthday, it's your birthday

If I die, bury me inside the Louis store (Ha, uh)

Uh

They ask me what I do and who I do it for (Yeah)

And how I come up with this shit up in the studio (Yeah)

All I want for my birthday is a big booty hoe (True)

All I want for my birthday is a big booty hoe (Tell 'em)..."

As 2 Chainz began to rap into the air, I looked up at the VIP where the birthday boy was stationed. He was already on the balcony, and he lifted his drink. *Damn, he cute,* I thought as I dropped my gown. I was still seductively watching him, but that changed in a split second. Zone walked over to the edge, and we locked eyes. *Oh, shit.*

I tried hard to continue and get my focus off him. I walked over to the pole and began climbing to the top. I stayed up there for a while and began to slap my ass. This brought me some time to look back up. However, when I did, he was gone. I slapped my ass one last time and flipped myself upside down. I eased down the pole slowly and landed into the splits. I was so out of it I didn't even pay attention to the crowd screaming and causing a money shower.

I looked over to Duke, our DJ, and spent my finger for him to go to the next song. I let out a soft sigh because it was time for my routine. H.E.R. "Damage" began to play as I seductively walked over to the black bag that held my cucumber. I grabbed it nervously as my mind raced to Zone. I quickly shook it off, then headed to the edge of the stage. Of course, Cletus was front and center with his money out. I slowly lay onto the ground on my stomach and pulled the cucumber to my mouth.

I looked Cletus in his eyes as I began to suck on it. Before I could go down, the sound of two gunshots echoed throughout the room and over the music. The sound of sparks from the DJ system made me look behind me, and the music had stopped. The equipment was smoking, and Zone was standing beside it with his gun in his hand.

I titled my head to the side because I wasn't processing what'd just happened.

Duke looked scared as hell, and the crowd of people began to run out of the club. I stood to my feet, and Zone looked at me with the most evil glare. My palms got sweaty, and my heart raced.

"Bambi, let's go!" His voice roared, and by the look on his face, I knew he was serious.

"Zone, what the fuck?" I asked, looking at him like he was crazy. Hell, he was crazy, but I was still trying to process that part.

"I ain't gon' say it again. Next time, I'mma shoot yo' ass."

I shook my head at his choice of words and looked down at all the money scattered all over the stage.

"Leave it," he spoke in an even tone, so I let out a deep sigh, annoyed.

I headed over to him, and he grabbed my hand. He led me out the door and right to his car. He opened my door and waited for me to get inside. He then walked over to the other side, and when I looked up, the boy whose birthday it was looked back and laughed. I shook my head and just sat there looking dumb. I looked out the window so I didn't make eye contact, but that was over shortly because Zone got dead in on my ass.

"Sharky's, huh?" he asked and chuckled, but I could tell it wasn't a friendly chuckle.

The car got quiet, and my pussy got wetter and wetter by the moment. Yes, the shit he just did was crazy, and I was glad Lorenzo wasn't there yet. Lorenzo acted like he was tough, but he ain't stand a chance against Zone. I also knew that tomorrow he would be making me pay for the equipment Zone fucked up, but he better had got that shit from the stage.

"I hope you giving me twenty-k because you fucked off my

money." I finally looked over at him, trying hard to piss him off.

"Bambi, shut the fuck up," he replied annoyed.

When we pulled up to his home, he quickly jumped out. I waited for him to open my door because if it was up to me, I wasn't getting out.

"Get yo' ass out."

I climbed out and headed for the door. I had only been here once, but I didn't care. I opened his front door like it was mine and headed up the stairs to his room. I didn't care if his girl was here. That bitch was gonna be sharing the bed. Since he wanted to act like he was my nigga, I was gonna treat him like my nigga.

I walked into his bedroom and began looking in his drawers for something to slide on. I was still in my damn two-piece. When I found a fresh white-tee, I slid it on with nothing else. I grabbed a pair of socks out one of his other drawers and slid them on. After about an hour, Zone still hadn't come up, so I lay in his bed. My buzz was gone thanks to his ass, so I was a bit sleepy. I laid my head into his goose-feathered pillows and closed my eyes.

Suddenly, he walked into the room, so I kept my eyes closed to pretend like I was asleep. From time to time, I snuck a peek at him as he moved around his room. He took his watch off, then began to strip from his clothes. I swear this man's body was so damn sexy. I almost gave myself away looking too damn hard.

"Yo' stupid ass ain't sleep."

"Fuck you," I wasted no time responding.

"Nah, fuck yo lying ass. I swear, my nigga, you a fucking liar."

"I ain't lie about shit."

"Are you fucking serious right now?" he asked and walked closer to the bed. He looked at me seriously, and I sighed to let him know I ain't have time. "Bambi you lied about where the fuck you work. Whole time, you a hoe."

"Nigga, I ain't no hoe."

"Shit, your profession of choice is hoe shit." He shrugged,

causing me to sit up.

"Well, I'm sorry, Zone, but everybody can't be drug deal-ers," I shot sarcastically. "Nigga, you don't know me, so don't judge my life."

"Bam, I don't need to know you. You a fake college student and stripper by night. The way you sucked that cucumber—nah scratch that. The way you suck my dick, I know a nigga taught you that."

I rolled my eyes and looked back at him. "Zone, why am I here? If I'm such a hoe, you could have left my hoe ass in the club. I had about twenty-g's on that stage, so you damn right I'll be a hoe to a nigga who don't wanna be in a relationship." I smirked, and he ain't have shit to say.

He looked at the wall and began to ponder my last state-ment. However, I knew Zone too well. He had some slick shit to come back with.

"Well, why would I want a relationship with a hoe?"

"Nigga, you didn't even know I was a fucking stripper. Ugh, I swear. Fuck you, Zone, with yo' confused ass."

"I ain't confused."

"Then tell me you love me. Tell me you want to be my nigga." I mugged him, waiting for him to say the words. Truth-fully, if he did, I wouldn't know how to reply. I guess this was my heart speaking and not my mind.

"Come on, Bambi. You already know what's up," he replied, pissing me off.

"Exactly." I fumed as I turned to my side, away from him.

The room fell silent, and I was in my feelings again. I swear this nigga got on my muthafucking nerves. He pulled this dumb ass stunt tonight for what? With nothing else to say, he got up from the bed and headed over to his dresser. I didn't know what he was doing, but when I felt something hard hit my leg, I looked over. It was a stack of money wrapped in a rubber band. He looked at me reluctantly, then walked out of the room.

Once again, Warzone's punk ass made a thug cry. Tears began to slide down my face as I looked over the money. For the first time, in a long time, it wasn't about the money. Fuck his money. I wanted him, and I wanted him in the worst way. However, after this, I swore to myself I was done with his ass. I wasn't about to keep letting him knock me off my square. I needed stability, and once again, he shut me out.

CHAPTER FOURTEEN

WARZONE

Two Weeks Later

"**N**igga, the fuck wrong with you?" I asked Baby Bro.
"Nothing."

"Man, something wrong. You running around this muthafucka with a long face. I know it ain't that bitch who got you bugging?"

"Nah."

"Lying, bitch. Nigga, then what is it? Football?"

"Man, it's her."

He dropped his head.

I looked at him without really knowing what to say. I thought about the night I tripped out at the club.

"So what she trippin on? Shit, you was just getting yo' dick sucked by her," I asked, fishing around.

"She prolly only did that because I was leaving to play ball. It was some out of spite shit because she ain't even let me nut."

Doobie and I looked at each other because it made sense. She only did it to piss me off.

"Baby bro, help me understand why you tryna hit the field when you got a bitch right there sucking you up? Not to mention, y'all was in Hawaii. One of the most romantic places in the world." Doobie said, looking at Zac like he was crazy.

"Man, what was I supposed to do? Not play?" Again, me and Doobie looked at each other. "When it comes to football, fuck her."

"And that's exactly why you looking like that now." I shook my head and headed for the door.

Doobie was right behind me, and we stopped on the porch. We looked at each other, and I knew Doobie had something to say.

"Baby Bro don't know what to do with her. This nigga chose football over head." He shook his head. "No disrespect, but Bambi fine as a muthafucka and too much for a young nigga to handle. That girl is a full blown woman, bro."

"On the real, she is," I agreed, looking out into the air.

"I say just snatch her. Keep it real, he ain't gon' give a fuck. You heard that little nigga. Football his life, which means Bambi ain't shit. You need to stop playing with that girl before one of these rich niggas recognize her worth and snatch her ass up out that club." He headed for his ride and hit the alarm. He looked back at me. "Go get yo' chick, nigga. I'll holla at you later. I'm going to see if Myra gives me some head. I ain't passing that shit up for nothing."

We both chuckled as he climbed into his whip. I stood on the porch for a hot minute and watched as his car drove by. Although I was watching the car, my mind was elsewhere. I thought about what Doobie was saying, and he wasn't lying. If the right nigga approached Bambi, it was a chance he'd snatch her pretty ass up. Lots of niggas didn't judge a bitch grinding in the club. I didn't judge her for it either. I was just mad she didn't tell me. Therefore, I threw the shit in her face and called her a hoe. I had to hurt her because a part of me was hurt.

Taking Doob's advice, I jumped into my whip and headed

for Bambi's campus. I really didn't know how this shit would play out because of our last day spent together. I could tell she was in her feelings again, and instead of catering to her heart, a nigga shut her down.

So here I was ready to redeem myself and tell her what she wanted to hear. I was at the point that if she rejected me, I was gonna make her stubborn ass submit. I had to make her believe me, so I was gonna be on some Keith Sweat shit. When I pulled up, I parked my whip in the second row of the parking lot. From where I sat, I could see her dorm, but I couldn't see the front door. I killed my engine and laid my head back to help ease my nervousness. I wasn't no Romeo, so approaching a bitch on some lover boy shit was out of my league.

Here goes nothing. I pumped myself up and opened my door. As soon as I did, I noticed a car's brake lights go on and off, and the sound of screaming got my attention. The sound was coming from the car, and as I listened closer, the girl's voice belonged to Bambi. I pulled my strap from my stash and ran over to the car at full speed. I yanked the door open, and my heart dropped when I saw Bambi's legs open and a man in between them. He was moaning and groaning while Bambi screamed for dear life with a pool of tears in her eyes.

My blood rushed through my body and attack was the only thing I could conger up. I hit the nigga in the back of the head with my strap, and he grabbed his head while turning around. I couldn't shoot him, too afraid I would hit Bambi, so I yanked his ass out and began hitting him continuously with the butt of my strap. I beat the nigga for so long he went unconscious. I pointed my strap at him and began flying bullets into his body. With every shot, his body jumped forcefully. I knew the nigga was dead, but I didn't stop.

"Zone!" Bambi's frantic voice called out to me and that was the only thing that brought me too.

I turned around, and our eyes met, and the shit only made me madder. I looked down at the geeky-looking dude, and as bad as I wanted to empty my last three shells into him, Bam needed me. I ran back over to the car and swooped her up. I took her to my whip and put her in the back seat. I jumped into the driver seat and wasted no time starting it up and pulling out the lot.

I wasn't sure about taking her to the hospital, so I drove her out to my crib. I drove so fast we were there in twenty-five minutes, less than normal. Again, I swooped her into my arms and took her into my home. I took her straight up stairs and into the restroom. I didn't know what else to do.

"Take yo' clothes off, ma," I instructed her as I helped her peel out her clothing.

She still had tears in her eyes, and the shit was killing me. Once I got her into the tub, I let her relax as I kneeled down beside her. I closed my eyes for a brief moment, trying to find the right words to comfort her. Instead of the normal thoughts I had, I spoke from my heart and not my mind.

"Bam, I love you, ma," I told her, and she looked over at me to see if I was telling the truth. I nodded my head to assure her, and I could tell I took her by surprise.

"I love you too," she replied and laid her head back.

"I'm so sorry this happened to you. I swear, baby girl, I'll never let another muthafucka harm you. From this day, you got my word to protect you."

A fresh set of tears began to pour from her eyes, and I knew it came from emotions. It's like, everything was happening so fast she hadn't gotten a chance to process it all. Just moments ago, she was being physically attacked, and her womanhood was being ripped from her against her will. And now, here I was, confessing my whole heart to her. I really didn't expect her to say much. All I wanted was her to believe in a nigga and relax.

"I know I been on some fuck shit, but not anymore. I'm not saying this because of what happened to you because I was already on my way to tell you I loved you. Ma, you mean more to me than you think you do. Now I feel like I failed you." I shook my head and dropped it, defeated.

"You didn't fail me, Zone. You're my hero," she spoke softly and sensually.

I let out a soft sigh because that shit meant a lot to me.

"Thank you," she added, but there was no need for thanks. I'd do it again if I had to.

"We just gotta figure something out," I told her, thinking about the cameras on campus.

Doobie's words began to play in my head, and just like last time, I did some shit without thinking. However, in a situation like this, a nigga ain't have time to think.

"Let me handle that," she assured me, and for some reason, she sounded like she had it under control.

I nodded once, although I knew I had to figure this shit out. I had to find a way to get rid of those damn tapes.

"Zone, I'm sorry for coming into your world and bringing you any drama. I just can't help it. I fell in love with you. I know what I'm doing is wrong, but it feels so right. I wanna be yours and only yours." She looked at me with the saddest, genuine eyes.

I nodded my head but remained quiet.

"I swear I knew you were a hoe."

I quickly turned around to the voice, and my heart dropped.

"Zac," Bam spoke, just as shocked as me.

"Nah, bitch, don't Zac me. So yall fucking?" He stepped further into the restroom.

"Man, Baby Bro, some shit just happened to her tonight, so it ain't the time." I tried to dismiss him. I didn't want him to find out like this, and it definitely wasn't the time.

"Oh, it's the perfect time. Answer the question, hoe." He walked closer to the tub, so I stood to my feet. "Bro's before hoes, huh?" Zac laughed like he was deranged.

I could smell the liquor on his breath, so I knew the nigga was drunk. When Zac got drunk, he got courage, so I knew exactly how this shit would play out.

"I swear bitch, I'mma kill…" He ran over to the tub and tried to attack Bambi, but I snatched his ass up and slammed him into the floor.

"Nigga, you know you can't win against me!" I shouted into

his face, reminding him that I would demolish his little ass.

"Taking up for yo' hoe. Get the fuck off of me and fight me like a man, bitch," he told me, now taking me by surprise.

Zac knew I didn't play that bitch word because wasn't shit bitch about me. Because he had just pissed me off, I had to set the nigga straight.

"That's the problem, you ain't no man. You a little nigga in a man's world. Maybe if you grew the fuck up, yo' bitch wouldn't want a real man. Yes, this my bitch and that head good as fuck too. Now get the fuck out my crib before I forget you my little brother."

I let the nigga stand to his feet, and I made sure to watch him. I swear on my mama, if he swung on me, I was gonna beat the breaks off his ass. We had a stare down for a few more minutes, but the nigga knew better. He looked from me to Bam, then back to me.

"You can have that hoe. I hope she break yo' heart too," he retorted, sounding like a little bitch.

I let the nigga have that, though. When he saw I ain't give him a reaction, he walked out with tears threatening to fall from his eyes. I stood still for a moment, and now, it was my turn to process it all. It definitely had to be a full moon out because this turned out to be one hectic night.

I took a seat on the toilet and dropped my head. I needed to gather my thoughts because like I said, I didn't want him to find out like this. I could see he was hurt, and on top of Bambi, who was hurting now, my Baby Bro had been scorned from this. *Damn*.

CHAPTER FIFTEEN

BAMBI

"When I was a little girl, I had this uncle named Ray who used to sexually abuse me a thirteen. He would make me suck his dick. Well, really he taught me how and would always tell me I had a gift. He made me think that exploiting myself and collecting money from it was the way of life, and that's how I became accustomed to using what I had to get what I want. I can't say I hate dancing because I love the adrenaline. I love the attention, and I especially love the money. On a regular night, I'd make at least five grand. On an event night, I'd make anything from ten to twenty."

"So do you..."

"I have." I dropped my head in shame. "Only the men who would pay top dollar. I would only suck their dick because by the time I was done with them, they wouldn't want nor have time for pussy."

Again, I dropped my head because Zone got quiet. I knew after this, he might judge me, but I had to let him in on my life.

I had never opened up to anyone about my life, so it was hard. However, it was my reality. My parents basically swept it under the rug now that my uncle was gone, but I had to deal with this forever.

"So this nigga who raped you."

"That's Cletus. He's just an obsession. He's the one who pays the most in the club. I've never sucked him up because all he ever wanted was for me to just dance."

His jaw locked, and I could see the frustration all over his face again.

"So what now, Zone?" I turned over to look at him.

"Shit, I don't know, ma. First, I gotta figure something out with that tape on your campus. Then, I'll worry about Baby Bro."

"What about us?"

"Shit, what about us? You mine now. Bam, I ain't going nowhere."

"So what about yo' girl and your mom?"

"I keep telling you that ain't my bitch. And as far as my moms, she gotta get over it like Zac. Bambi, don't nobody run me or my life. Yes, it's a fucked up situation, but shit happens, and we grown. Get some rest, baby. You got a flight early in the morning." He kissed my forehead and pulled the covers back.

It's been three days since the rape, and everyday, Zone had me right here in his crib, in his bed. He would only leave to get food or check his traps. Other than that, we spent our days just lying around talking. For the first time tonight, he asked why I was stripping. And for the first time in my life, it felt good opening up. Tomorrow, I was going to my parents' for a few days, so I was gonna miss the hell out of him.

"I'mma miss you, ma." He looked me in the eyes and said it as if he were reading my mind.

"I'mma miss you too. You gon' behave while I'm away?"

"Of course." He smiled on the sly, then chuckled. "I love you." His face got serious.

"I love you more." And just like that, he pulled me into his arms and rested his chin on my head. I knew I was gonna be out soon because being with Zone felt like a dream. It felt like I was meant to be here, and we were destined. "Good night, babe." I closed my eyes, and within minutes, I fell into a deep slumber.

***

"Bambiiii!"

My mother shouted my name so loud the entire airport turned to look in her direction. She ran over to me with open arms, and I fell into her chest.

"Mommy, I missed you guys. Where's Dad?"

"He's in the car. Grab your luggage. Let's go."

She grabbed one of my suitcases and pulled my arm. We headed out of the airport, and my dad was right there waiting. When he noticed us, he jumped out the car and hugged me tightly.

"My baby girl." He smiled and looked at me to see if anything changed.

"I missed you too, Daddy." I smiled.

"You picked up a little weight."

"I've been eating like crazy." I giggled because I did pick up a few pounds.

"Lets run along. Your mother has her dinner cooking in the slow cooker."

He grabbed my luggage and took it to the trunk of his car. We all climbed in, and as soon as we pulled off, my mother excitedly began to tell me all the things she had planned for us to do. Everything she blabbered about sounded fun, but I wish I was back home with Zone. Thinking of Zone, I pulled out my phone to text him.

Me: *Hey.*
I waited for his text as I made small talk with my mommy.
Zone: *Sup, baby. You landed?*
Me: *Yes. I'm with my mom and dad now.*
Zone: *Okay, good. A nigga miss yo' ass.*
Me: *(smiley face) I miss you more. I can't wait to get back home to you.*

Zone: *I'll be waiting.*
Me: *Wyd?*
Zone: *Just got to mom's crib. She texted me saying she needed to see me.*
Me: *You think it's about Zac?*
Zone: *More than likely.*
Me: *Okay, well, you behave, Zone. (smirk face)*
Zone: *I told you I ain't trippin off that girl, ma. I'm waiting on you.*
Me: *Okay. I'll call you later. Love you.*
Zone: *Love you too.*

    I put my phone in my purse and sat back with my thoughts all over the place. Ugh, I knew loving Zone was gonna be hard because I didn't trust him at his mother's house. She and Meka were pretty close, and from the looks of things, that's where she spent most of her time.

    Zone swore he wasn't fucking with her, but that was bullshit. They were just laid up in Hawaii. Because he now referred to me as his girl, certain things were off limits. If he wanted to keep me around, he was gonna have to keep his dick to himself. Meka already didn't like me, so now, I knew she hated me more. Therefore, I definitely knew she would try to prove I wasn't shit by fucking him.

CHAPTER SIXTEEN

WARZONE

When I walked in my mom's crib, Zac was the first one I spotted sitting on a stool near the kitchen. Because my mother was close by, I knew they were discussing me, but I didn't give a fuck. This shit was childish as fuck, and I was gonna remind my moms I wasn't a fucking child. As soon as I walked into the kitchen, Zac mugged me, and my moms shook her head.

"Ma, I know you ain't call me over here about this little nigga."

"Damn right, I did. Have a seat."

"Nah, I'll stand. I got shit to do, and this ain't it."

"What you gon' do is watch yo' fucking mouth. You coming in here slick talking like what you did was cool. Well, it's not Warren. That's your damn brother. I can't believe you."

"Ma, I didn't mean for the shit to happen, but that nigga don't want her."

"So that means you're supposed to sleep with her?"

"Well, yeah. Shit."

"You've lost your damn mind. You need to leave that hoe alone."

"Why she gotta be all that?" I replied, looking at Zac. I knew exactly what she meant, and I knew he ran his mouth like a hoe.

"What are you gonna do with a stripper? You got a good girl upstairs crying her poor eyes out over you, and you just keep hurting that girl."

"I don't want Meka, and you know that. You the one keep forcing that girl on me."

"You don't want her why because you don't wanna be in a relationship? Yet and still, you go starting one with a damn slut. Zac told me he heard you telling that girl you love her."

"And that's my muthafucking business." Again, I mugged Zac as I shook my head. "So you want yo' bitch back?" I asked him sarcastically.

Whether he said yes or no, he wasn't getting Bam back and that was that. When he didn't reply, I knew it was because his ass was too embarrassed to say. I shook my head again because the nigga wanted Bambi back, and it was evident in his eyes.

Just as I was about to add some slick shit, Meka emerged from the back, and I could tell she had been crying. A part of me felt bad, but fuck that. Meka wasn't my bitch, and I wished everybody would get that through their fucking heads.

Meka walked past me, to the fridge, and she tried her best not to look in my direction. My mom looked from her to me, and I could see the disappointment in her eyes.

"Leave that girl alone, Zo, Zone whatever them knuckleheads call you in the streets."

"It's Zone. Warzone, to be exact. Ma, please stop fronting for these two. Y'all ain't bout to dictate what I do with my dick. I'm a grown ass man who holds this whole fucking family down. So take yo' son in the back, and give him yo' tittie. He looks hungry."

I turned to walk away, shocking the hell out my moms. I didn't mean to disrespect her, but they all had me fucked up. I paid the bills around this bitch, and they were coming at me like I was a fucking kid. Like I said, Zac ain't know what to do with shorty.

They were on some college shit—meanwhile, baby shaking ass in the club. In my eyes, Bambi was much more than a college sweetheart; she was wifey material. She was mature, sexy, and had a head on her shoulders. She was just misguided by the fortune. I ain't like the decisions she made in life, but I was gonna change her lifestyle. I was gonna put her in a crib and help her with whatever career goals she had, but first, I needed to see where her head was at.

Before I made it out the door, I looked back at Zac, then my moms.

"And to set the record straight, I ain't leaving Bambi alone. That's my bitch now, and if he wants her back, he can take her back." And just like that I walked out.

I caught the pain in Meka's eyes before I turned completely around to leave, but that shit wasn't working. When I got outside to my whip, I climbed in, and the first thing I did was call Bambi. I held the phone to my ear and waited for her to answer.

"Hey, babe." Her voice graced the phone, and it brought me to ease. This was all I needed to hear.

"Tell me you love me, ma."

"I love you, Warren," she replied, and her calling me by my government name really told me I wasn't making a mistake.

"I love you too. I'll hit you later."

"Boy, no the fuck you not. Yo' ass ain't bout to just call me sounding like you just had a full blown war, make me say I love you, then hang up. Now what's up?"

I couldn't help but laugh at how lil' mama came at me. Shit was cute as hell, and I could tell she was serious. I started my engine and fell into a deep conversation with her all the way to my trap. I told her everything that had gone down, and I could hear the jealousy in her voice when I spoke on Meka. I had to assure her that no matter what my mother said, wasn't shit between me and Meka happening. I could tell she believed me, but I could also hear the doubt in her voice. At this point, all I could do was show her.

CHAPTER SEVENTEEN

BAMBI

"Your soul, your flow, your youth
Your truth is simply proof we were meant to be
But the best quality that's hookin' me
Is that you're loving me for me, is that you're loving me for me..."

I moved around my room singing to Christina Aguilera's "Loving Me For Me." I was bored as hell waiting on my mom to finish cooking. I was missing the fuck out of Zone, and dealing with the thoughts of Cletus was hard. Every day, that shit still bothered me, and I even had fucked up dreams about it. Never in a million years would I have thought Cletus would get down like that. Nigga pulled some straight Myron from Players Club shit on me. I couldn't believe he raped me because of my expectations of the thugs and hood niggas that visit the club.

Ring...Ring...Ring...

I looked down at my phone, and it was Lorenzo. I had been dodging his calls, and I knew eventually I had to speak with him, so I decided to answer.

"Hello?"

"Bambi, I'm really disappointed in you."

"Don't start yo shit, Zo."

"The fuck you mean? You and yo little boyfriend shot my damn club up, and now people are scared to come here."

"He didn't shoot the club up; he shot the equipment." I rolled my eyes in annoyance. "Does it matter? I left all the money I made there, so that should cover it, plus more."

"Damn right, I got that. Now tell me about Cletus."

"What about Cle?"

"I'm not sure. They found his body on a college campus; your college campus. I'm sure you know something. Cletus being dead is a big deal because he spends lots of money here."

"I don't know shit about Cletus. And is that all you think about? Your damn club and money?"

I shook my head. I swear this nigga ain't care about shit. Not his wife at home, his children, or none of the four other baby mamas his old dried up dick had. You would think a man making the money he made hustled to take care of their family, but nah, not Zo. He ain't do shit for none of them kids outside of his marriage. He barely took care of them too.

"You know what it is with me, Bambi. You knew this when you came to the club."

"Well, guess what? Fuck you, and fuck your club because I quit!" I ended the call furious. I thought about Cletus raping me, but I couldn't tell him.

"Bambi, the food is ready. Come get cleaned up so you can eat." My dad opened my door and stuck his head inside.

"Ok. Thanks, Dad." I bit into my lip, afraid of asking him. "Ummm, Dad."

"Yes."

"I need a really big favor." I looked up from the bed and tried to give him my innocent face.

"What's that, sweet pea?"

"Is it possible that you can confiscate a video tape of a

shooting so someone won't get in trouble?"

"Do what?" he asked as if he didn't hear me, but I knew he did because of the frown on his face. "Bambi, what have you gotten yourself into?" He stepped into my room.

"Nothing, Dad, I swear. Promise you won't get mad?" Instead of responding, he looked at me, ready to curse my ass out. "A friend of mine helped me out and got into some trouble. A shooting happened." I dropped my head, too afraid to look up at him. The silence confirmed he was angered, so I didn't speak.

"You know damn well I can't do that! Are you trying to get me to lose to my job? Bambi, I didn't pay all that money for you to associate yourself with those types of people. Now you're gonna tell me who this friend is, and we're gonna turn him over."

"I'm not turning him over!" I jumped to my feet. He had me fucked up if he thought I was turning Zone over.

"Oh, yes, the hell you are! It's not up for discussion, dammit!" He fumed with spit flying out his mouth.

We had a cold stare down, and he was definitely serious.

"What's all this yelling about up here?" My mother walked in looking between me and my dad.

"Your got damn daughter out there hanging with thugs, committing crimes."

"What? Bambi, is this true?"

I looked at her ashamed, and I didn't know how to answer.

"You hear your mother talking to you."

I looked at him, then my mother.

"Just forget about it," I replied and stormed past them.

I went downstairs to get my plate because I refused to sit at the table with them. When I tried to grab it and walk off, my father was heavy on my heels. He began shouting down my throat, and it hurt me more. He didn't know the story and was already ready to lock our asses away. I sat my plate down because I had lost my appetite. Not only that, but the excitement of being with my parents was now gone.

I waved him off and headed for my bedroom. I began packing my clothing because a bitch was out of here. I knew if I stayed,

I wouldn't hear the end of this. My mother was a mute, so her saving me from my father's hurtful words wasn't even gonna happen. Therefore, I chose to leave.

After packing my belongings, I headed back downstairs, pulling my luggage. When I reached the last step, my father was gone, but my mother stood there with tears in her eyes. I could tell she wanted so bad to encourage me to stay, but instead, she nodded her head.

"I love you, Bambi. Please call me when you make it."

I nodded my head okay as tears began to fall from my eyes. I headed for the door without looking back. I was too afraid my father would try to make me give him the info on Zone. I stepped onto the front porch and pulled out my phone to call a Lyft. After, I texted Zone to have him pick me up from the airport.

In his text, he asked what happened, but I chose not to say. I slid my phone into my fanny pack and walked up the street a few feet from the home. Another few tears fell from my eyes because my vacation wasn't supposed to go like this. I missed my parents, and I was hoping we could catch up. I guess I thought wrong.

CHAPTER EIGHTEEN

WARZONE

I watched Bambi as she pranced around in the mirror. For the first time, she was wearing something sexy but elegant, and it made her look classy with so much damn sass. Tonight, I wanted to take her out on a night in the town because I wanted her to get her mind off of everything going on around us.

Her parents had pissed her off, my mother was still tripping, and I knew the situation with the nigga that tried to rape her still bothered her. Last night, before we went to bed, she was bugging out about the possibilities of me going to jail. She seemed so worried it put a lot on a nigga's mind.

I had to assure her I was gonna be okay and promise her that I wouldn't leave her. I refused to leave Bambi out in this cold world because in my eyes, I was all she had. It's like, the world was against us, so it was us against the universe.

"Bring yo' sexy ass here." I stepped closer to her and pulled her by the arm. I took her into my embrace and looked in the mirror with her as I held her close to me. "You look pretty as shit, baby girl. I like this look on you."

"So what you saying foo?"

"I'm saying you look sexy but elegant, with yo' ratchet ass."
I slapped her on the ass.

"You talking bout me dressing ratchet, but you doing
ratchet shit by slapping me on the ass." She smirked and moved
out of my hold.

"Shut yo' ass up. You *my* little ratchet. Now grab yo' shit so
we can go."

"Yeah, I'mma show you ratchet."

She smirked again and hit me with that sexy ass giggle
that meant she was gone' blow my socks off. I shook my head
and walked out because my dick grew effortlessly. That shit was
crazy that the mention of some head from Bambi sent a nigga in a
frenzy. My dick had a mind of its own, and her fire ass pussy ain't
make shit no better. The way we were fucking, it didn't surprise
me when she told me she missed her period. Me, I figured her ass
was pregnant, but her personally, she didn't believe it.

I headed for the limo and climbed in so I could plug my
phone up and call my moms. Today was her birthday, and I hadn't
talked to her since she tripped out on me. I knew she was still
upset, and I really ain't care, man. However, I couldn't just say
fuck her for her day. I let out a soft sigh as the phone began to ring.
When she answered, she didn't seem too excited to hear from me.

"Happy birthday, Ma."

"Yeah, yeah, thanks," she replied, and there was silence.

"That's all I wanted, Ma. Love you."

"Love you too. We're having a barbecue this Saturday. Come
on by, and leave yo' huzzy at home." She hung up before I could
reply.

I shook my head and laughed at her pettiness. My moms
knew she missed me, but just like me, she was stubborn as hell.
Her stubbornness was what caused every man to leave her, which
was why her ass was lonely now. I knew that could have been my
story, but I got my shit together, and fast.

Look at me now. For the first time, I felt genuine love. No, I
wasn't in love, but with Bam, I saw it coming. We still had some

growing and getting to know one another. There was never a limit to learning the person you planned on spending the rest of your life with. Bambi was full of surprises, so getting to her was enjoyable. She was fit to be my queen, and after shaking her old ways, I could see myself with her for longevity.

"Where we going?" Bambi asked, climbing into the car.

"Just out on the town," I replied and handed her a glass of Ace I had just poured. She took the glass and took a sip, then sat back to enjoy the ride. Before I knew, it we were pulling up to Antonica's Vinyard and Winery. It was a very elegant and peaceful atmosphere, and it was perfect for a mental escape.

I helped her get out the whip and we walked up the small hill. It felt good to have Bam's arm wrapped into mine. It really felt good going on a normal date like normal people did. This some shit I never got to experience. Like I said, I've never had a girl.

Hell, I didn't know where to take her. That wasn't the norm. I googled romantic places for couples, and this was one of the choices. Knowing Bam had a real corny side, I knew she would like it.

"Awww, baby," she squealed and turned around to face me.

Just like I thought, she liked it. From where we stood, you could look down into the vineyard, and it looked like a forest. Because of the large barrels of wine and the many grape vines, Bambi knew exactly where we were.

She ran over to me and gave me a kiss. She then grabbed my hand like an anxious child and pulled me inside. I loved seeing her like this. She was excited as hell, and her eyes beamed one of a child. Knowing Bambi's story, she missed out on a normal childhood, and it was evident in her eyes. Any time she saw things exciting, she would light up.

"Oh, yeahhh, I'm bout to get fucked up!" She did a little dance and walked over to the first vine.

"Do you, ma. It's your world."

"Awww, thanks, babe. I love you so much."

"I love you too. Now let's taste some wine." I kissed her forehead.

Bambi had a nigga's mind at ease right now. I wasn't gonna let shit fuck up our day, especially because I had to break the news to her that mom's barbecue was coming up, and she ain't have a choice but to attend. I knew she was gonna be mad, but I ain't give a fuck. Bam was mine now, and these people had to start accepting it one way or another.

CHAPTER NINETEEN

BAMBI

"I can't believe I let you drag me here." I climbed out of Zone's 2020 Maserati nervously. I looked around the yard, and when I saw the crowds of people, I began fidgeting.

"Man, stop tripping, ma. If they can't accept you here, then they can't accept me. We leaving this bitch." Zone grabbed my hand and pulled me towards the home.

We walked into the gate, and the smell of barbecue lingered in the air. My stomach began to growl, and it dawned on me that it was nearly one p.m., and I hadn't eaten.

"Can I just wait out here?" I asked Zone before he had a chance to step into the house.

I really didn't feel comfortable being here, so going into Ms. Vandiver's home made me fidget.

Instead of replying, or letting me stay out by the pool, Zone tugged at my hand and pulled me inside. The first person we spotted was Meka. She looked from Zone to me and rolled her eyes.

She didn't bother to speak, so I didn't speak to her.

Ignoring Meka, we headed into the kitchen, and it was full of people. His mother went to speak until her eyes landed on me. Her arm dropped and fell on her thick hip as she looked at Zone like he'd lost his mind for bringing me.

"Happy Birthday again, ma." He kissed her cheek, but she continued to watch me.

"Happy Birthday," I spoke politely. Although her birthday was Tuesday, the celebration was today.

Instead of her replying, she frowned her face and looked at Zone. "You hard-headed as hell." She began shaking her head and dismissed him.

Just as I was gonna tell him I'm going outside, Zac walked into the kitchen. *Oh, Lord,* I thought, knowing it was gonna be some more bullshit on top of the bullshit going on now.

"I'm gonna go outside." I nudged Zone and slid my hand from his.

I walked out of the home before he could disagree. When I made it outside, I let out a breath of air, happy I had escaped them people. I found an empty seat on the two-seater swing and began swinging as I watched everyone around me.

A few kids played in the yard, and a few people enjoyed the swimming pool. The yard wasn't too packed, but there were enough people for barbecue. I knew this was because Zone didn't fuck with many people. He also implanted it in his mother's head to stop letting the world know where she laid her head, so I was more than sure everyone was family.

"Here, ma."

I looked up, and Zone was walking over holding a water and grape soda wrapped in a napkin.

"Thank you." I faintly smiled, still feeling out of place.

"Stop looking like that, Bam. I keep telling you, ma, you belong to me now, and fuck whoever don't like it. If you wanna leave, we can...." he went to speak, but something distracted his thoughts.

I looked in the direction of where he was looking and my

eyes landed on Meka. She was giggling hard as hell, and she sat next to some dude. She mouthed something to him, and when he reached over to kiss her, Zone's jawline flexed with anger. I watched him as he watched her, and the shit was pissing me off.

"Babe, I'm hungry." I tried to pull his attention from Meka.

"Huh...oh my bad, shorty. Let me holla at my unc."

He walked over to the man who was on the grill and said something I couldn't hear. They began to talk, and from time to time, he continued to grill Meka. A part of me got jealous because why was he tripping on his ex? Yes, I understood the disrespect because this was his mother's home, but to my knowledge, they were never in a relationship, so she was free to do as she pleased.

After talking with his uncle and stalking Meka, Zone walked off towards the home. Shortly after, his uncle brought me a plate. I looked down at it and was ready to eat, but I had no fork. *Damn*, I cursed because I either had to wait for Zone or go get one myself. I stood up from the swing and made my way to the home through the back door. When I walked in, Zone's voice echoed through the home, and he sounded enraged.

"It don't matter, Ma! Do you know this nigga?"

"It's really none of your business who she has around here! She doesn't belong to you! Yo' hoe outside waiting on you, so you need to attend to her!" his mother yelled at him.

"Meka gone always be my bitch! That hoe gone always belong to me, Ma! And don't worry about Bambi! She ain't your concern!" Zone shouted back at her, and the room went silent.

When I didn't hear anything else, I turned to walk back outside because I had heard enough. My appetite was gone, and my feelings were so fucking hurt. Hearing him say she would always be his bitch kinda fucked with not only my ego, but my heart. Here I was thinking I was doing enough to keep this nigga locked in, but hell nah. I wasn't doing shit. He was still in his feelings over Meka, and after today, no one could tell me different.

I took a seat back on the swing and got lost in my thoughts. When Zone finally walked out of the house, he came to ask me was I straight. I could tell he didn't know I heard everything he said because if he did, then he'd know right now I wasn't fucking him. I wasn't gonna show my true colors, so I kept everything he asked at a yes or no.

I couldn't wait to leave because when we got back to his home, I was gonna grab my shit and just go. School started back this Monday, so I was gonna stick to my normal routine. Zone insisted I went to school from his home and give up my dorm, but that would never happen. I was gonna always keep my dorm for just in case purposes like this one.

***

"I hope that nigga dog you out and break your heart."

I quickly looked up, and Zac was standing there holding a bottle of Don Julio. Perusal, his ass was drunk and talking out the side of his neck. I rolled my eyes because his choice of words were definitely some shit a childish ass boy would say.

"You need to go in there and check on yo' nigga. He's prolly eating the ass off Meka."

Hearing him say that pissed me off more because I hadn't seen Zone in about an hour. Meka had pretty much disappeared and her company left, and I was sure because he was uncomfortable.

Zac began laughing like shit was funny, and just as I turned around to curse his ass out, Zone walked out of the house. When he spotted Zac in my face, his face frowned, and he stormed over to us.

"The fuck you got to talk to her about, my nigga?" He pushed me behind him and stepped into his face.

A part of me wanted to save Zac because I knew what Zone would do to him. However, because of all the shit he was just talking, I let him deal with that shit. I stood right behind Zone, although I was upset with his ass too.

"Ain't nobody said shit to the hoe."

Crack!

Zone's fist crashed into his chin, and he instantly went stumbling back. He grabbed his jaw and looked at Zone as if he were deranged. He couldn't believe what had just happened, but that was dumb because he asked for it.

"Tell him what you just told me. About how he was inside eating Meka's pussy. Tell him, Zac." I rolled my eyes and looked at Zone. Before Zac could reply, I was in on his ass. "So is that what you were doing?" I stepped over to him so I could slap his ass if need be. All these niggas was scared of him, but I wasn't afraid of Zone.

"Hell nah. You gon' listen to a little bitch like Zac?"

"You tell me. I mean, she's gonna always be your bitch, right?!" I shouted, and he just looked at me.

He was stuck because he knew those were his choice of words, and just for that, I was getting far the fuck away from him. I stormed out of the gate and power walked past his car. I heard him calling my name, but I kept moving. When I heard the sound of his car door slam, I took off running and cut through the side of someone's house. I quickly hid and waited for his car to pass, and when it did, I jumped the back gate and ran full speed.

I didn't stop running until I was out of the area. Knowing I was safe, I stopped to take a breath of fresh air. I began to think of how dumb it was for me to run when the nigga knew exactly here I'd go. Shit, I had nowhere to go but my dorm, and I was sure he would come looking for me there.

CHAPTER TWENTY

BAMBI

"**B**ambi, you have to see him one day. He's been by here four times." Gio jumped from the sofa to say.

"I'm good, G. I came to grab my notebook." I headed into my room.

I could hear her shouting from the living room, but I was trying to hurry before Zone popped up. It's been three days, and I was doing a good job at ignoring his ass. Since I only had one class this semester, I was able to dodge him coming to my classes.

One day, the Dean called me into the office, but I didn't go. I knew he either wanted his shorty, stubby dick sucked, or Zone was looking for me. Ever since I had been Zone's girl, the interest in being spitefully pleased by dean or Mr. Fox was no longer a thrill. The dean didn't sweat me, but Mr. Fox had begun acting like a total jackass.

He was acting so much like a bitch that I was ready to drop his class. The nigga had the audacity to question my relationship with Zone. He even threw Zac in my face. In so many words, I he was calling me a hoe because of them being brothers. But I wasn't a hoe when he wanted me.

"Mr. Fox?" Gio asked, so I stopped to look at her.

"Hell yes. Nigga getting annoying."

"I knew he was in love with your ass." She giggled, but right now it wasn't funny.

Gio got a kick out of my life. And although we didn't talk like that, it was things I still felt the need to fill her in on: like Zac and Zone.

"Girl, Mr. Fox better gone somewhere." I headed for the door. "If Zone comes, tell him I went to my parents' house."

"It won't work, but I'll try." She lifted from the sofa to come lock the door.

I headed out and sighed heavily on my way to Mr. Fox. I cursed myself the entire way because I definitely didn't wanna be bothered.

When I made it to his class, the projector was on, and the lights were off, so I tried my best to sneak in. I took my seat and pulled out my materials so I could catch up. Every now and then, my mind would travel to Zone. Therefore, I continued to look back every chance I got.

I knew he would catch my ass eventually, and when he did, I was prepared. I couldn't front, I missed his ass like crazy, but fuck that. I wasn't going over board. The shit he said was foul, and the question that lingered in my mind was, did he in fact have feelings for Meka?

He swore he wasn't fucking with her. He swore she wasn't shit to him, but after the way he was looking when he saw her with dude, that shit had cap. That nigga loved her, and my second question remained, how can a man love two women?

"Excuse me, but can I help you?" Mr. Fox stopped in the middle of his lecture.

Everyone looked in the direction he was looking, and my heart began to thump. "Damn," I cursed under my breath because the nigga was staring dead at me.

"Bring yo' ass here, Bam!" His voice echoed through the room.

Mr. Fox didn't look pleased, and Zone didn't look like he gave two fucks about my teacher. "On Denise, don't make me come get you," he spoke again.

When he said that, I knew he meant business. Denise was his grandmother who had passed several years ago. He always told me how their relationship was stronger than he and his mother, and he even had her name tattooed like, three times. Therefore, at the mention of her name, I shaped up.

I let out a small sigh as I lifted from my seat. I grabbed my belongings and headed out because I only had twenty minutes left for the class. I walked towards Zone, and I could feel the fury coming from Mr. Fox. I ignored his ass, too scared that if I looked his way, Zone would pay attention. He wasn't dumb by far, and Mr. Fox clearly didn't care at this point.

"Your grade is depending on this project," Mr. Fox said, just as I made it to the door.

I turned to look at him and nodded my head okay. I quickly turned around and walked out and right past Zone. I stormed to my dorm with his ass right behind me.

"I swear you gon' make me beat yo' ass." He yanked me by the arm, causing me to spin around.

"The fuck! Don't touch me." I snatched away from him and stuck my key into the door.

When I walked in, I slammed the door, knowing he would catch it, but I felt the need to be disrespectful. I headed into the kitchen to fake get something to drink. I knew if I went in my bedroom, the possibilities of me coming out my clothes were slim to none. It never failed with Zone.

The nigga kept my pussy wet, which was why I was in this damn situation now. I knew I was pregnant, but I wasn't gonna confirm it with him. I blew him off anytime he mentioned it, and now that all this happened, I was contemplating an abortion.

"Yo, you trippin, ma. Ain't shit with Meka that you think."

"Nah, it ain't what I think. It's more."

"Ain't shit more." He shook his head once and looked at me. He stood with his hands in his pockets, and his head tilted to the side. I kept trying to turn my head because the nigga was so damn fine. I knew I would give in. "I know you might not believe me, but the last time I smashed her was Hawaii. Bam, I ain't been fucking with Meka because of you. Although she never was my bitch, I still kept Meka close to me and fucked her when I felt like it.

"You also gotta understand, I'm the nigga who hold Meka down. I pay all her shit, so if she fucking another nigga, then that nigga can pay her shit. Like I said, I apologize for what you heard, but I don't want her, ma. Just give me a chance to show you, a'ight"

He stepped closer to me. He looked me in the eyes just as he bit into his lip; talk about pussy wetttttt.

"I've never had a girlfriend, so all this shit is new to me. I really apologize for hurting you, and if I have to stay away from mom's crib because of her, I would. For you, I'll do that."

"You don't have to do that, Zone," I whispered and tried to look away from him. "Do you love her?" I finally looked him in the eyes, demanding he told the truth.

"Honesty?"

"Honest, Warren."

"I love Meka, kinda like family. Like, the way she is with my moms and little brother makes me not have a choice but to love her. No, I don't love her like I wanna be with her. I guess I never really prepared myself for if I found love, for Meka and I's relationship would affect my relationship. After seeing how hurt you were, it killed a nigga, so I knew I had to cut Meka off. I have a lot of love for Meka, but I can't put her feelings before yours. I chose you, Bam."

Again, he stepped closer to me and was now so close our lips were almost connected.

"You love me?" he asked demandingly.

I nodded my head *yes* because my emotions had me caught up. He reached down to kiss me, and I was happy we were in the damn kitchen. I closed my eyes defeated, not wanting to give in, but everything he said sounded so damn convincing. The way he grabbed me, the way he demanded I listened to his every word, and I guess him being here spoke volumes. If Zone was still on his bullshit after this, then I was gonna leave him for good.

CHAPTER TWENTY-ONE

WARZONE

"Where you going?"

"I gotta go to my dorm, Zone."

"Why, yo' ass ain't got class?"

"I know, but there's a pep rally at the school, and my friend Gio is performing."

"Oh, okay. So my little sister gon' be there?" I chuckled, and it took her a minute to catch on.

"Yes, the entire football team will be there."

"A'ight. Well, give me kiss."

"No, I'm still mad at you."

"After all this dick I been putting on yo' ass all week, and you still tripping?"

"Yes. Boy, you ain't off the hook that easy. I love you, now bye." She bent down and finally kissed me.

I slapped her on the ass and watched her walk away. A part

of me wanted to go back to sleep, but because it was one in the afternoon, I decided to just get up. I began making a few calls, then called the nigga Doob. I knew he would be excited about the prep rally, and he was gonna get all the homies together. Next, I headed for the shower so I could get my day started. As soon as I was climbing in, I got a text.

Mek: *You did all that just to say fuck me again. I just don't get it, Zone. You don't want nobody else to have me, but you don't want me.*
Me: *They can have you, ma. Nice life…*

I was done with playing games with Meka. After the shit that went down at mom's crib and the way I hurt Bam, I was gonna keep my distance. Therefore, whoever wanted Meka could pretty much have her.

***

Saying fuck it, and deciding to go up to the school for the pep rally, we walked in at least fifteen deep. I knew Zac wasn't gonna be pleased to see me, but he'd be happy we came. He still fucked with my crew of niggas because they were always like big brothers to him.

Because we were late, there were no seats available, so we stood in the front. The band had the rally turnt up, and the first person I spotted was Bam's dorm mate. Seeing her told me Bam was around here somewhere, so I began skimming the crowd for her. When my eyes fell onto her, it's like she felt my presence because she looked right over at me. I hit her with an eye wink, and she instantly blushed. She made her way over to me, and I pulled her into my arms.

"Attention, Cougars!" one of the staff members stepped up to the mic and began talking.

"This bitch," Bam said, looking at the woman who was speaking into the mic.

She rolled her eyes at the woman, and it made me laugh because it was some catty campus drama.

"I love you crazy, girl. When you taking yo' ass home?"

"I am at home."

"Man, get fucked up, Bam. I'mma roll out with Doob. I'll be home about one. Yo' ass just better be there."

"Okay. So where's my key?" she asked with a smirk.

Little did she know, I was already ten steps ahead of her. I pulled them from my pocket and swung them in the air.

"Oh my God, Warren. You really got me keys?"

"Hell yeah, ma. I told you ain't no games being played. You my soon-to-be wifey and bout to give me my first seed." I smiled and kissed her forehead.

She shot me with that innocent smile, and like always, that shit melted a nigga. Bam was hardcore as fuck, but the way she melted for me turned me the fuck on. It made her seem submissive to me, and that shit stroked my ego.

"You love..." I went to speak, but the chatter of the crowd grew.

Bam and I looked around, wondering why was the crowd so in awe, and that's when our eyes focused on the huge projector. I didn't know what type of shit this college had going on, but this wasn't health class, and a porno was playing.

This chick was on her knees inside of one of the classrooms, while a man, who appeared to be a teacher, leaned on his desk getting some electrifying head. When the camera zoomed in, I noticed the dragon ass tattoo with the trail of flames, and it looked like Bam's ass tatt.

I looked down at her, and she was watching the screen as her hand hovered over her mouth. I looked back at the screen, and the moment I did, I almost lost it. I had a clear view of Bambi sucking the life out of her professor's dick. The same professor whose class I had just snatched her ass out of.

I looked over at her, and tears were pouring from her eyes. I was so shocked; I didn't know what to say. My mouth was open, and I looked between the screen and Bam. This had to be a dream or a joke. Hell nah, it was reality because the way that man's eyes

rolled   to   the
back of his head, he was definitely getting that magic throat from
my bitch.

My blood started boiling, and I swear if we weren't on a college campus, I'd shoot this entire school up.

"I'm sorry, Zone." Bam tried to step over to me and grab me.

I snatched my arm from her grasp and began shaking my
head at her.

"Damn, you really a fucking thot. You let everybody slide
babies down yo' throat." I continued shaking my head, and now
all eyes were on us. This shit wasn't only foul—it was embarrassing as fuck.

"Zone, I could explain."

"Explain? Explain what? The proof is in the fucking video.
Or should I say, throat? On Denise, don't ever say shit to me
again." I stepped up on her. I wanted so bad to spit in her face, but
instead, I grabbed her arm and snatched my keys out her shit.

"Zone, please!" she cried out but them tears wouldn't help
the embarrassment.

To make matters worse, my little brother sat across the
field with a huge smirk. It's like he got a kick out of this and that
told me he was the one behind it. I swear I couldn't even be mad
because his actions weren't what caused Bambi to be the hoe she
was. The nigga found something to get revenge on her, so he did.

The shit was sick if you asked me, but this was how the
game went. I could only imagine how embarrassed he prolly felt
getting his bitch snatched by his big brother.

I swear for the first time, I felt foolish. The pain and embarrassment I felt—Bam wasn't worth it. If I could give this nigga
back his bitch, I would in a heart beat, but it was over.

I turned to walk away from Bam and even left my niggas
behind. I headed for my car, and just as I made it, I caught the last
glimpse of Bam running into her dorm sobbing uncontrollably.

Like I said, their tears didn't matter. At this point, I wanted
that bitch out my life, to kill that seed, and stay the fuck away
from me. It was over.

CHAPTER TWENTY-TWO

BAMBI

I t was day two of the end of my life, and I literally felt like my life had come to an end. I didn't know if I was hurt because of the limit of revenge, or was the worst part the embarrassment I caused Zone. I spent the last two days in my dorm crying my eyes out, too damn embarrassed to call. I knew that eventually, I would have to face him, so I decided to get up and go.

It was four-thirty in the morning, and I knew by the time I got there, it was going on five a.m. Zone was an early bird, and he normally got up at six a.m.

I sluggishly got out of bed and brushed my teeth. I then slid into a pair of sweats and my Cougars college hoodie. I made my way to my car, and when I started my engine, I had to take a breather. I was nervous as hell, and my anxiety was kicking my ass. I really ain't know what the fuck I would say because the fact remained, I was caught.

I knew Zac and Mrs. Fox were behind it, and I knew that because of the devious looks they both gave me. I swear I wanted to punch the fuck outta her, but just like Gio said, I was in the wrong. It was all my Karma coming back to haunt my ass for fucking over Zac and messing with a married man. The fucked up part was, I hate Zone had to get dragged into this, although he played a helluva part in all this.

"It could've been right, but I was wrong (Uh)
Only think 'bout you when I'm alone (Yeah)
The part of me that cared is almost gone
And I know that I can't get caught up..."

Once I got the willpower to leave, I pulled out of the lot and headed for Zone's crib. My entire drive, I prepared myself on what I would say, but I knew the words wouldn't come out right. I swear it seemed like I got there faster than I normally did. A bitch ain't have time to get her thoughts together because the normal forty-minute drive actually took twenty minutes.

As soon as I turned the corner, the illumination from squad cars bounced off the homes and lit up the entire block. There were a swarm of police cars along with a swat truck. I knew I wouldn't be able to get through, so I went to make a U-turn.

Just as I turned around, I saw Zone being escorted from his home in cuffs. I slammed my car in park and jumped out. I ran at full speed, and the moment I got in front of his home, a few officers grabbed me.

"Zone, baby!" I began crying as they held me to keep from getting to him. "Let me the fuck go!" I tried to slither my way from their hold.

"Chill, Bam. I'm good, ma." Zone spoke calmly, but I didn't give a fuck. He was good, but I wasn't.

"Zone, I love you." A new set of tears began to pour from my eyes. I wanted him to understand that no matter what, I loved him. Just as they were putting him into the squad car, our eyes locked.

"Love you too, ma," he responded and nodded once.

"Bambi, you get your ass from over here!"

I turned around to a familiar voice. When our eyes met, I couldn't believe that my father stood there. It told me he was behind all this. What was really a trip was the plain clothing he wore, which told me this was out of his jurisdiction. I couldn't believe he had gone this far to arrest Zone, not knowing what the hell was going on.

I ran up on him, and the other officers approached us, but he waved them off.

"She's my daughter," he assured them, so they backed off and began moving around.

"I'm not shit to you." Tears poured down my face. "I really can't believe you. You know this is the reason I don't fuck with you now and hadn't fucked with you since a child. It was never about me. It was always about your job. Just like when Uncle Ray was molesting me, you didn't care how mentally it fucked me up. All you cared about was throwing that man behind bars and proving to the force you were the head officer. And now look. You take the one man that actually loves me and locks him away for some shit you don't even know about!"

"He's a damn murderer. Cletus Frazier." My father held up a picture of Cle as if he was proving a point.

I looked at him and the picture, and I couldn't contain myself. I spit a fat ass loogie at the picture, and it barely missed my father. He looked at me as if I was crazy, and I matched his energy.

"Well, guess what, daddy? Your victim ain't a victim; he's a damn suspect. Zone took that man's life because he tried to rape me. He tried to fucking rape me!" I burst out into tears.

All my emotions from my childhood until now had come back. I couldn't even control the hurt nor anger. My father stood there looking pale-faced, and all I could do was shake my head. I turned to walk away from him because I couldn't stand to look at him another two seconds. Right now, I hated that man, and him

115

birthing me didn't mean shit.

Just as Mrs. Fox and Zac, my father had now become my enemy. It was fuck them, and I swear I wasn't gonna get revenge. I was gonna give it to God. The only man I loved was now behind bars, but I was gonna do what I could to get him out.

***

I sat on the metal seat and looked through the glass at my own reflection. I took short breaths to try and coach myself out of my nervousness, but it wasn't working. The moment Zone stepped into my view, he looked down at me and chuckled once.

He then took a seat and grabbed the phone that was connected to the wall. The entire time, he hadn't taken his eyes off of me, and this shit made me more nervous. Neither one of us spoke; we both just looked at one another, trying hard to muster up the right words to say.

Finally, I decided to speak because this nigga was making me second guess coming to visit. Although he told me he loved me, he still gave me that look as if he was disgusted with me.

"We're having a baby," I spoke and bit into my bottom lip.

He paused slightly, and I knew he was searching for the right words that wouldn't hurt me. I knew Zone too well, and that nigga spoke his mind, especially when he was angry.

"How come you ain't tell me yo pops a cop?"

"What?"

"Exactly what I said, Bam. Yo pops a fucking pig, shorty, and I don't fuck with pigs."

"I'm so sorry. Please believe me when I tell you I don't fuck with him either. Zone, I don't really fuck with my mother because of him. After this, I'm really cool."

"After this? Ain't no after this. I'm done for, and thanks to that bitch ass nigga."

"No, you're not, Zone. I swear I'm gonna get you out of here."

"I don't need you to do shit but handle that." He nodded his head towards my stomach.

I looked at him because he had to have lost his damn mind.
"What you mean handle it?"

"Handle it. I love you, Bam, but I'm good. First you, humiliate me, then look where I'm sitting because of you. I promised myself they would have to kill me before I ended up back here, and now look. But I'm a gangsta, shorty. I got this. You handle that, and take care of yourself." Again, he nodded and stood to his feet.

I quickly jumped to mine and tried hard to stop him.

"Zone, please, I'm sorry. Baby, everything from my past is just biting me in the ass. I swear, I never meant to hurt or embarrass you. Please just give us a chance."

"Shit, I ain't got nun'. My life over, ma." He dropped his head and turned to walk away.

"Wait! If I get you out, will you give us another chance?" I asked with tears now cascading down my face.

He looked at me, and I could tell he didn't believe there was a way, but instead of him doubting me, he nodded his head yes. This melted my heart a bit, and when he walked away, I was left with just me and my thoughts. I had to figure it out and fast. Zone and I had an entire future ahead of us, and our love was destined. By any means, I was gonna do what I could. And if need be, I'd sacrifice my life for his.

CHAPTER TWENTY-THREE

WARZONE

It was the day of my trial, so a nigga's emotions was all over the place. It had only been six months because I chose to do a speedy trial. With speedy trials, you had to be cautious because sometimes, you wouldn't give your attorney enough time to discover evidence that could help your case.

However, I ain't give a fuck. I was tired of going to court every morning, so I wanted this shit to be over with. So far, they had nothing but a tape from the 911 call when Cletus' body was found. They also had an anonymous tipper who gave them my name, and after investigation, everything led back to me. The trip part about it was, Zac was the voice that played on that tape, and I knew the nigga's voice from anywhere.

My mother, who sat in this very court room today, swore it wasn't him, but like I said, I knew that nigga's voice from anywhere. Not once did Zac step foot in any of my court dates and that alone told me he was guilty.

I know y'all thinking why would he, but fuck that. A bitch ain't enough to say fuck my life when it was being judged by twelve. Speaking of, I hadn't seen Bam, but I talked to her about three months ago. She thought I was playing when I told her I was good. Let her tell it, she killed my baby as I asked, so there were really no strings attached.

I made sure to have my attorney reach out to her and tell her to dodge the police, and that way, they wouldn't make her get on the stand. I didn't wanna take the chances of Bambi fucking up my case because her testimony would definitely injure me.

"Your Honor, I would like to call my second witness, Bambi Davenport, to the stand," my attorney spoke, making me damn near yell.

I watched as Bam emerged from the hall, and my eyes landed on the baby bump in front of her. *Lying bitch*, I thought, because her stomach was huge.

She wobbled her ass onto the stand, and my attorney began asking a series of questions. Bambi told everything that happened that night except me pulling the trigger. Once my attorney was done, the DA began questioning her, and I knew this was the ultimate.

"So Ms. Davenport, are you saying that Mr. Vandiver wasn't on the scene of the crime at the time of the shooting?"

"No, he came after."

"So you are telling this courtroom today, and you swore under oath, that you are the one that pulled the trigger?"

"Yes, sir," Bam spoke confidently into the mic, shocking the hell out of me.

I shook my head because this girl had lost her damn mind.

"What is she doing?" I reached over and whispered to my attorney.

"She's doing a damn good job. That's what she's doing."

"I have no further questions, Your Honor," the DA said, and my attorney stood up.

"Ms. Davenport, can you explain one more time your reason for shooting this man."

"He tried to rape me." Bam sighed into the mic. She looked at me, then quickly turned her head.

"Your Honor, I object. There's no evidence of that."

"Mrs. Gascon, do you have evidence of this happening, because you're not gonna accuse a dead man of rape in my courtroom."

"Yes, I do your honor," she spoke, and the entire courtroom gasped. She walked over to the judge and handed him three documents.

"Your Honor, exhibit A is the DNA that was given by Andre Davenport, the head of FPD. This sample is of findings from Mr. Cletus Frazier's groin of Ms. Davenports DNA." As soon as she said it, the DA dropped his head because he knew this case was over.

After my attorney went over a few more exhibits that helped me, I knew we had this shit in the bag. I looked at Bam, and I couldn't do shit but shake my head. I then looked over and locked eyes with her father. When he winked and nodded his head once, I sat back in my seat, feeling like a million bricks had been lifted off my shoulders.

A nigga wanted to cry like a bitch right now, but I kept it G. It's like everything had worked in my favor, and I swear it was God, and He was right on time. I couldn't do shit but ask Him to forgive me for the sins I committed hurting my little brother. I also thanked the Lord for Bambi, who was giving me my first blessing. I watched her as she got off the stand, and when she neared my seat, she looked at me.

"I love you, Warren. Just remember, for you, I will," was all she said, then walked out.

I really didn't understand the meaning of that, but I was sure it had something to do with her going out on a limb for a nigga. Man, after this, I owed not only Bam but her pops my life. Just like that, my life could have been taken from me, but in that same breath, it was giving me a brighter future. I swear after this, I was changing my life around because this was my third chance at life.

"Oh, and she wanted me to tell you something about you promised," my attorney whispered in my ear, breaking my concentration.

I smiled hard as Bam's words played in my mind. *"If I get you out will you give us another chance?"*

"In a heartbeat, ma," I spoke out into the air, meaning every word.

After this, it was only up from here. I was gonna raise my seed, get my family back in my good graces, and even forgive Zac. nothing in the world was gonna stop me from being the best husband she deserved. I was gonna put her past behind us and move forward.

Damn, I couldn't wait to feel my little Throat Baby's mouth wrapped around my dick.

The End!

Visit My Website
http://authorbrbiescott.com/?v=7516fd43adaa
Barbie Scott Book Trap
https://www.facebook.com/groups/1624522544463985/
Like My Page On Facebook
https://www.facebook.com/AuthorBarbieScott/?
modal=composer
Instagram:
https://www.instagram.com/authorbarbiescott

Made in the USA
Monee, IL
16 July 2021

73741007R00069